SUGAR PLUM BLISS

Book 4.6, A Bliss & Neil Christmas Short

A CORNWALL AND REDFERN MYSTERY

GLORIA FERRIS

Table of Contents

GENRE: Mystery/Thriller & Suspense/Police Procedural/Humour
SUGAR PLUM BLISS
A Cornwall & Redfern Mystery
Book 4.6 A Bliss & Neil Christmas Short
First Edition
ISBN: Print 978-1-7388692-5-1
ISBN: ebook 978-1-7388692-4-4

"Computers make excellent and efficient servants, but I have no wish to serve under them."
(Mr. Spock, Star Trek Season 2 – Episode 24 1968)

Written in Canadian English

For more information, contact gloriaferriswrites@gmail.com
Editing: Donna Warner djwarnerconsulting.blogspot.com
Cover Design: MJ Moores, infinite-pathways.org
Cover Images: Deposit Photos

CAST OF CHARACTERS

Bliss Moonbeam Cornwall	*You could say she runs the town*
Police Chief Neil Redfern	*Bliss' husband*
Chico Leeds	*Lifelong friend of Bliss'*
Louis	*A bartender Bliss hires for the Gala*
Devon	*Clerk at Canadian Tire*
Marshall, Adrian, Colton, Reagan	*The four teen volunteers*
Mr. Archman	*HS principal, not seen but heard*
Mrs. Blackman	*Secretary of St. Mary's Church*
Sgt. Thea Vanderbloom	*Member of Lockport PS*
Lonnie and Brandon	*Members of Search & Rescue team*
Winnie	*Owner of nail spa*
Piper	*Bartender & Louis' girlfriend*
Pan	*Glory Yates' housekeeper*
Fang Davidson	*Lifelong friend of Bliss'*
Glory Yates	*Mayor of Lockport*
OPP Det-Sgt Tony Pinato	*Glory's love & Neil's best friend*
Father Hanley	*Priest of St. Mary's Church*
Jake and Freddie	*Paramedics*
Dr. Ed Reiner	*Coroner, surgeon, OB/GYN*

Say Hello to the Friends You Know

I PICKED MYSELF OFF the parking lot in front of my car and brushed the snow off my coat and jeans. Would it kill Chico to have his staff come in a few minutes early after a storm and clear the lot for customers? At least get Christmas shoppers inside the building before the slippery tile floors dumped them on their asses. Bliss Moonbeam Cornwall could not afford a broken bone. Too much to do.

I nearly made it to the entrance, but my ringing phone distracted me and I fell on my butt, staying where I was while I fished my phone from my tote. It was a text from my manly, blond, hunk of hotness, known to the town of Lockport as Police Chief Neil Redfern. We were four months married but the magnetism between us had only intensified, despite our many differences. For instance, he enjoyed the Christmas season and I tried not to be too humbug about it.

Bliss, where are you?

CT pkg lot. Wr r you? Leaving most of the vowels out of my messages usually threw him off my track.

How did you get out of our driveway?

Amed fr gtes nd flrd it.

There was a moment of non-activity. What's that sound? Are you playing Christmas Carols in your car?

As if. I was on the ground close to the automatic doors. Every time I moved my arm, the doors opened and closed. When it opened, the notes of *Have a Holly, Jolly Christmas* rolled out. Quite entertaining, other than the music.

After a few more nonsensical questions about my whereabouts, he disconnected. He wanted very badly to tell me to go home and stay off the roads but he was too smart for that.

I got to my feet again, the back of my jeans soaked through to my skin, and lurched into the cart area where I grabbed one that was sure to have a wobbly, squeaky wheel. Using it for balance, I made my way safely across the wet floor and pointed the cart at the swinging barricade, the purpose of which nobody knew. My cart had four squeaking wheels.

Other than the wheels and the carols, perfect timing. Last night's storm forced shoppers to stay home for an extra hour to shovel out their driveways. I was pretty much alone in the vast store. First on the agenda, find my buddy, Chico Leeds.

Being the owner/manager, he did as he pleased which meant he usually hung around the paint department and re-filed the little sample chips discarded by shade-challenged customers. Trouble was, Chico, like many men, had trouble with blues and greys. As a result, the blue section looked like a Roman mosaic bathhouse. An occasional lavender chip caught the eye, like an interior decorator elf worked all night to make it pretty.

He stood behind the paint counter sorting a pile of grey chips, frowning in concentration. A green garland decorated with red balls draped across the counter. Red and green. Big yawn. "Hey, Chico."

He jumped a foot, and his handful of sample chips flew from his fingers and landed by his feet. "Bliss. What are you doing here?"

"Uh, shopping. I need decorations for the First Responders' Christmas Gala tomorrow night. You promised to come and take pictures." Chico was a skilled, amateur photographer and we usually had loads of fun at social functions with his camera and my photogenic-ness.

"I remember. Don't *you* forget to bring my cheque."

I spoke to the top of his curly head since he was on the floor picking up bits of paper. "Glory signed the cheque and you'll get it at the party. I'll keep it safe in my shoe."

"I'd rather you store it in your bra. Did Glory include a seasonal tip?"

"Have you met her?" Glory Yates was the mayor of Lockport, and I worked as her part-time assistant as well as running my own cleaning business and a few side hustles, like on-line shopping for an exclusive clientele who appreciated designer handbags and shoes. Glory might be wealthy, but you know what they say — the rich don't stay rich by giving away their money. Even if the money came from the taxpayers. Glory belonged to that club. "Don't worry. I'll set up a tip jar."

"What do you want? Kind of late to be buying decorations for a Christmas party tomorrow night. Not that I want to talk you out of buying more, but you bought a lot of stuff last year for the greenhouse party. Why don't you use those?"

"That belongs to the greenhouse and will be used again next week for the community food drive after the parade. The First Responders' budget is coming out of the town coffers, so I'll need a good deal."

"Can't help you there, Bliss. This is the first week of December. Christmas paraphernalia won't be marked down until the 22nd. Except for the odd loss leader. You can check the weekly flyer for the sales." He spread out the pile of grey chips on the countertop and moved them around. A splash of blue peeked from under his right shoe, but I didn't mention it.

"Are you arranging those by shade? Don't they have sequential numbers?"

"This is easier. The seasonal display is behind you to your right. You can't miss it."

If I stayed in the store much longer, listening to Yuletide music, I'd go elf-crap crazy. "The sooner you help me choose my décor items, the sooner I'm out of your hair."

Chico parked his glasses on top of his head. "Best offer I've had since you walked in. Let's get at it."

Fall On Your Knees

HE TOOK OFF SO FAST, I lost him in the wreath aisle. Did I need a wreath? Maybe for the front door of the church hall. I'd wait and see what discount Chico gave me.

The cart was so freaking huge, I could load up a set of winter tires and a school bus battery, and still have room for a new microwave. I didn't need any of those items, just some stupid Christmas junk to make the firefighters and cops feel seasonal.

"Chico!" If he ran out on me, I'd hunt him down if it took all morning. I raced up and down the aisles, pushing my empty cart around corners without, I suppose you could say, following the store's "reasonable care policy" on the operation of a wheeled death machine.

I located Chico at a junction where a careless staff member had parked a display stand of Christmas-themed socks. I spotted a black pair with elves cavorting across the heels and cuffs, and threw them into my cart for Neil. He'd probably wear them on Christmas day while he opened the special present I got him — a military-grade drone. That's what it said on the box.

Chico darted into a main aisle and I swung the front end of the cart to follow. The only other customer in the store popped up beside Chico and they fell to the floor in a tangle of legs and arms.

Seriously, not my fault. The store should have more than a one-size-fits-all cart. I would've missed them both with a smaller model.

They crawled aimlessly on their hands and knees like dying hornets in October. I backed up to give them room to stand. The hapless shopper grabbed the cart to pull himself up. Chico stayed down and felt around for his glasses. I picked them off the floor and handed them over.

A high-pitched version of *Silent Night* morphed into a spirited rendition of *Holly, Jolly Christmas*. Didn't I just hear that one on my way in? The men each clutched a side of my cart for support and I wasn't going anywhere.

"Can't you get your staff to turn the volume down on that racket?" My eardrums throbbed, as did my right eye when I recognized the clumsy shopper. Louis Something, the bartender from The Wing Nut Bar and Grill on the highway. I'd hired him for tomorrow night. I pretended not to notice him rub his thigh like he was hurt. It was too late to find another bartender.

"When people pile in here, it gets noisy. The volume is set for a store filled with merry Christmas shoppers." Chico polished his lenses on his company shirt and addressed Louis. "I'm terribly sorry, sir. I do hope you aren't hurt."

See, right there. Chico as a business owner should know better. Apologizing is tantamount to admitting culpability, leading to legal issues and insurance claims. "He's fine. Right, Louis?"

He looked down at me. "Bliss. What a surprise. I think my spleen is ruptured from your cart. Otherwise, tip-top. How about yourself? Not hurt, I hope?"

Luckily, I was fluent in sarcasm. "Great! I'm okay, too, I think. A bit shaken, but I'll be fine. Don't give me another moment's thought." Pretty sure your spleen isn't in your left leg, buddy.

Sheesh, the guy had to be six foot four and weigh 200 pounds. A tank could run him over and his spleen would give it the finger. With his dark hair, blue eyes, and square jaw, Louis would be a hit with the women at the party, the main reason I hired him. My other choice was a thirty-something blonde. Piper was the proud owner of super-perky bosoms, either one of which was bigger than both of mine. I didn't want the firefighters and cops — the ones with testosterone — hanging around the bar all night.

Chico looked from me to Louis, catching on. "Okay, well, as long as we're all fine. Bliss, you have some shopping to do, I believe. Maybe I can help this gentleman find something?"

Chico's wife rarely let him out of the house — or the store — without her, so it was entirely probable he never got chatty with Lockport's bartenders. "Louis, this is Charles Leeds, the proprietor of this wonderful establishment that plays Christmas Carols all the ding-dong day from the morning after

Halloween until somebody threatens to burn the store down mid-January. Charles, this is Louis, the new bartender at the Wing Nut Bar and Grill. Have you ever been there?"

Chico shook Louis' hand and side-eyed me. "Tiger and I go to the Wing Nut quite often. On our monthly date nights."

I turned my snort into a cough. "Monthly date night? That's so special." Tiger was her real name, digging her claws into Chico in grade 12 and never releasing them. Sad, really. We had good times with our friend, Fang. Before Tiger. However, I shouldn't judge him. He and Tiger were parents to three over-the-top, indulged, darling children. Must be hard to get away from them.

I grabbed Chico's sleeve, "You're helping me. I'm sure Louis knows his way around a gigantic hardware store. Right, Louis? Oh, if you're in the Christmas section for festive socks, there are some cute ones right here. I got the dancing elves for Neil."

He backed up. "No socks. I got turned around. I'm looking for tools, I guess.

I hung onto Chico while he directed Louis to Aisle 17 where he would find power drills. A present for Louis' dad.

I waved Louis on his way, after reminding him the church hall would be open for him to set up as early as 5 p.m. tomorrow evening. "Bring lots of imported beer," I called after him. "Firefighters love that stuff."

Oh, No, the Mistletoe!

"FIRST, I NEED SOME hanging balls," I told Chico. "If you run out on me again, I'll go to customer service and have you paged until you come back."

"Okay! What colour?"

"Not red or green, or silver or gold. And definitely not pink."

He pointed behind me. "That leaves light or dark blue. A combo would be pretty. We have a few boxes of navy left. Very popular this year."

"Ick. I don't want popular. I have a colour palette in mind. Do you have anything in plum?" The store was filling up. On the far side of the store, a newborn baby screamed its lungs out. You know, that note that almost breaks the sound barrier. Between whiny, shrieking kids and the blasting, blasted music, I had one nerve left. Even that shorted out when *Good King Wenceslas* started up.

"Purple?" He looked around the shelves as though he didn't know what was on every square inch of shelving in his store. "There we go. On the top shelf, against the wall."

I looked up. Purple, plum, same thing. "I'll need five boxes. Can you climb up and get those for me?"

Chico co-opted a young clerk, Devon, to fetch a ladder and get me five boxes of twelve, three sizes per box. Would sixty balls be enough?

I visualized the twelve-foot tree in the church hall, and garlands strung everywhere. Glory said she wanted the hall to look magical. "Another three boxes, please," I instructed Devon. "Plus, five of the white, for contrast."

I asked Chico, "Can I return what we don't use?"

"As long as the items are in original packaging with appropriate tags, and you have the receipt, yes.

I quickly scanned the top shelves, not seeing anything else I needed. "Thank you, Devon. That will be all. Not you, Chico. I'm not done." King Wenceslas wound up his endless, snowy, Christmas Eve stroll and next up was *I Want a Hippopotamus for Christmas*.

I decided that green garlands would look best with the plum and white balls. I threw a dozen into the cart which, amazingly, was filling up fast. "White lights that don't twinkle, and I guess that's it."

Gauging how many feet I needed, I added twelve boxes of lights to the heaping cart. That wiped out the stock on the shelves and Chico called Devon back to fetch more inventory from the storeroom.

Chico halted at the end of the aisle, causing the cart to connect with his butt. "What about a mistletoe ball We could have some fun with it at the party. Take photos of people kissing, either their own spouse or someone else's."

I glanced between the cheap plastic ornament and Chico. "We don't need that kind of behaviour to start fights between cops and firefighters. Trust me, you'll have plenty of photo opportunities, planned and spontaneous. Blackmail-worthy, even."

Chico confiscated the cart, citing too many children who could come to grief under the wheels if I drove. He said those exact words.

"Stop!" Behind boxes of tiny manger pieces, I spied a stash of plum-coloured Santa hats. The staff member who hid them was going to be very upset at the end of their shift today. Probably wanted them for their own party. "Score. I'll take the dozen." Seeing the hats with the manger gave me a great idea.

"Anything else, Bliss? It's getting busy in here and there are other customers I can be helping."

"Let's go by the hardware section. I need a nice hammer to smash your music system to bits."

"We use a commercial service. Good luck convincing the corporation you took out the sound equipment in a fit of Grinchiness. So, if that's all, I'll take you to the register and park your cart for you."

"You need to stay with me and discount the items as we give them to the cashier. Like we did last year when I bought the stuff for the food drive event."

He shook his head like he was my disappointed grandfather. Or, Santa. "What is wrong with you? What in actual frick is going on in your brain? Do you think I live to serve you and give you discounts?"

"I'll pay full price for the socks."

He ran over two kids on the way to the checkout. Just their feet, but my eardrums honestly popped at the sound they made. I was held up for ten minutes while Chico gave the kids free animated puppets and baseball-sized lollipops from a wire stand near the checkout. By the time he mollified Mom with a — free — miniature, fully-decorated Christmas tree, I was ready to head to the register and never mind the discount. He refused to release the cart.

Before escaping to his paint corner, Chico told the cashier to give me a 15 per cent discount, 5 percent less than last year, but he didn't disallow the socks, so that was a bonus. I was glad I didn't pick up a wreath, though.

Louis was in the next lane over. He refused to acknowledge me when I yelled a greeting.

I was a bit worried he was angry about the mishap that wasn't my fault, and not show up tomorrow night. I should google if certification and a police check were required to serve liquor at a private event.

I rubbed my sweaty hands on my jeans and handed the cashier a town credit card. I might be on deck to tend bar and I doubted I could pass the check. Or, to put it another way, the chances of my husband handing me a police pass to mix drinks were less than Frosty's butt remaining frozen during a January thaw.

I dragged my laden cart through the unplowed parking lot, followed by the mournful voice of Elvis singing *Blue Christmas*.

Bless All the Dear Children

"THERE ARE SUPPOSED to be six of you. Who's missing and when will they get here?" I pointed at each of the four teenagers clustered around the doughnut box I brought in from the car. I had three boys and one girl at my disposal for the next four hours.

"Drake and Edna couldn't make it," the girl told me, yawning to show her boredom.

Edna? Who names their kid Edna in the 21st century?

"They didn't want to be here," the taller boy amended.

"None of us want to be here," the girl snapped. "It's Friday. I have three videos to upload."

I sat behind a wooden table in the foyer of the St. Mary Immaculate church hall and pulled a packet of stick-on name labels and a pen toward me. "You four will do admirably. Give me your names and I'll write them on these labels for you to affix to your shirts." I didn't have time to match faces to names especially since they all looked the same with straight, shoulder-length hair and lumberjack shirts. Although the girl wore false eyelashes. "I don't care if you give me fake names. That just means I can't sign your forms to take to school on Monday."

At the blank stares, I picked up the forms paper-clipped together and placed Drake's and Edna's face down. "Let's do it this way. Who's Marshall?"

A cherubic-faced teen with reddish hair and stubble around his jawline stepped forward. "Me. I'm named after Eminem. Marshall is his real first name."

"I've heard of Eminem." I liked the rapper's style. He swore a lot, and he didn't rap Christmas carols that I'd knew of. I wrote the name on a label and handed it to the kid.

I repeated this three times. As well as Marshall, I had Adrian, Colton, and Reagan, the latter being the girl. With their back to me on ladders and tables, hanging up decorations, I wouldn't see their names, but it was a control tactic. Now, I had their identities. And, I had their forms. To sign or not to sign.

"Do we have to stay until four o'clock?" Colton asked. He was the tallest kid, good for getting up there into the corners.

"If you want your forms signed, yes. If everything is done to my satisfaction a little early, I don't see why we can't come to some agreement. You want your community service hours served before year end, don't you."

Wow, you never saw such a quartet of huffy teenagers as I faced after my totally innocuous statement. Which part offended them?

Reagan soon told me. "We are not on community service. That's for persons convicted of crimes. You know, the ones in orange jumpsuits you see picking up trash along the highways with an armed guard."

"Okay." I think this one watched too many reality cop shows from the US of A. "Sorry, I misspoke. You aren't court-mandated to be here."

"Ma'am, in order to graduate, we have to complete 40 hours of community involvement activities." Adrian smiled, showing off lime green braces. "Volunteer hours."

Ma'am? I'd be keeping an eye on this one. "Got it. We didn't have to do that when I was in high school. We helped out in the community because we were responsible, caring quasi-adults."

"You're getting paid now, though, right?" Reagan asked, flapping her two-inch lashes at me.

"And, you're not," I responded. "One more thing. Hand over your phones."

Over the babble of protests and actual tears forming in Marshall's eyes, I waggled the forms at them. "It says so right here. I'm to hold onto your phones until the job is done, or you're given a break. In that case you may access your phones for fifteen minutes. Check if the world still spins without your help. Let's go, people. We have lots to do. Let me repeat. If the job isn't completed satisfactorily in ..." I checked my phone, "Three hours and forty minutes, I do not sign the forms."

Ever so slowly, they passed three iPhones and an android to me. I placed them carefully into my tote and handed Reagan my keys. "First up. You, Adrian, and Marshall go to my Matrix in the parking lot and bring in the ornaments. One trip should do it. Colton? Try and find a step ladder and bring it into the hall. There's a utility room beyond the kitchen."

Alone in the foyer for a few minutes of blessed silence, I texted Neil.

Brng fd fr dnnr.

You want me to bring home food? Too tired to go out? Any requests?

Ht & sxy, lk y. Kddng, nt spcy.

Nothing spicy? Got it. See you later.

We usually went out for Friday dinner. Not tonight. Every restaurant in the land would be playing Christmas Carols, generally the jingly ones featuring animals — reindeer, chipmunks, hippopotamuses, geese ...

I should have encouraged the three teens to make two trips. A couple of boxes fell off the teetering piles. They didn't slow down, kicking the boxes ahead of them across the snow towards the door. Were the ornaments plastic or glass? Chico would never allow me to return broken ornaments.

I stood up and reached for the door to yell at them when the silence was broken by a sonic boom. What the frack!

The sound originated from the back of the hall. Did Colton blow himself up?

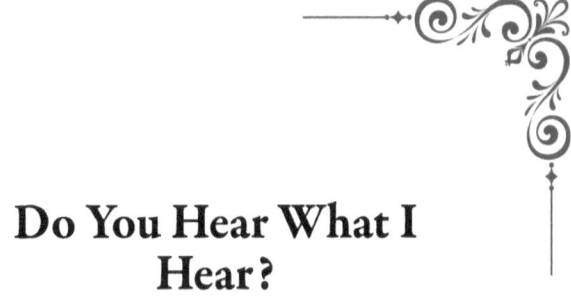

Do You Hear What I Hear?

I LET GO OF THE DOOR and ran through the foyer into the hall, my hands clapped over my ears. No debris or smoke. The noise morphed into *The Twelve Days of Christmas*, complete with violins and tubas. Currently, 10 lords were a-leaping, so almost done.

"Colton!" Where was that kid? Please, don't let him be unconscious or bleeding. I should have checked the fine print for liability before taking possession of 'volunteer' helpers. "Colton." I continued through a kitchen that was as white and clean as you'd expect in a church facility. Nothing had exploded in here.

He staggered out a door between the double-doored fridge and the stove, and shouted at me. "Holy shit. All I did was press a button for the music. Some streaming crap equipment. Never saw such old technology. I pressed all the right buttons, but the noise won't stop. That's gotta be 100 decibels. We'll be deaf if we stay in here."

"Come with me." I grabbed his arm and we raced out of the kitchen. He pulled ahead in the hall and beat me to the foyer where the noise level abated somewhat but not to comfort level. At this rate, the entire population of Lockport would be evacuating, thinking the power plant just outside of town was issuing a warning of impending nuclear disaster.

We snatched up our coats and joined his buddies in the parking lot. The twelve drummers were wrapping it up but, to my horror, the song looped around to the lone partridge in a pear tree. Who should I call? Police, fire department, Ministry of National Defence? My head buzzed from the noise and I couldn't think straight.

"Can we have our phones back?" Adrian asked.

"No." With their phones held hostage, they were less likely to disappear on me. How could I explain to the high school principal that I lost four of his volunteers at the same time? Mr. Archman had been my math teacher in Grade 12, and I refused to listen to his sarcastic rebuke the rest of my life. *Why am I not surprised, Ms. Cornwall, that you were unable to hang onto six of my students for a few hours? What's that you say? Only four showed up? Are you sure you haven't simply misplaced them? I sent you six.*

Assistance came from two directions. The church secretary, Mrs. Blackman, steamed around the corner from the priest's parsonage, rectory, whatever, her face like thunder. A pickup truck cornered into the parking lot on two wheels, then slowed seconds before it took out five innocent bystanders and a white-haired matron whose expression didn't bode well for Bliss Moonbeam Cornwall.

Thumpety Thump Thump

LOUIS JUMPED FROM THE cab of the truck. "What's that noise?"

I explained as much as I could between gritted teeth. "Colton, here, engaged a button in a closet in the kitchen. He couldn't shut it down."

Mrs. Blackman got down into my face. "This is unacceptable, Mrs. Redfern. I don't know how you accessed the media room, but it's supposed to be locked. The sound system is not in working order, and we're expecting a technician next week. That is the reason we encouraged you to engage a disc jockey for your event tomorrow night."

Colton stood beside me, shaking his left leg while holding his hand to his right ear, like he took on too much water during a swim meet. "My head is thumping," he said loudly.

I needed to shut this down now before the circling lawyers landed. If Colton went deaf, it was his own fault, and I refused to take the blame. The high school shouldn't release substandard students into the volunteer pool. I could only hope, for the sake of society, that these four were not our future.

"Colton." He shook his right leg and pressed the alternate ear. I grabbed his hand. "Stop it."

He did stop but shook his head and wiggled his fingers in both ears. "My head is stuffed."

I spoke loudly into his face. "Your hearing will return." With any luck. "Why did you go into the closet? Did you find a ladder?"

"No! No ladder. But I saw the old streaming equipment and figured we needed some music or even a radio. Deadly dull, that silence is."

Okay, we established the sound heard round the County was Colton's fault. "Was the door to the closet locked?"

"How could I get in there if it was locked?"

Good point. I turned to Mrs. Blackman. "How do we turn it off?"

Her faded blue eyes widened and her mouth tightened. "I have no idea — pull the wires? This is not acceptable. The room is supposed to be locked. One of our committee ladies must have forgotten. Still, there was no reason for anyone to go in there."

Louis pulled a long canvas bag from his truck bed. "If you're willing, I'll try and disable the system. I've bartended here before, so I know where the media room is."

Mrs. Blackman and I looked at each other. She was wild-eyed and breathing heavily. Sharp pains pierced my eardrums and my head throbbed, not unlike the discomfort from too many Christmas Carols, but worse. Much, much worse.

I handed Louis a pair of foam ear plugs from a baggie in my tote. "God speed, Louis," I told him. Mrs. Blackman pressed the back of her hand to her mouth and waved him off.

We waited. And, waited. A police car pulled up, and my friend, Sergeant Thea Vanderbloom, walked up to us. I told her what was what, and we were joined by a rescue van from the fire station. Two responders jumped out, equipment bags in hand. Lonnie and Brandon according to their name tags. I knew them both but, geared up in helmets, hearing protection, mics and radios, I couldn't tell who was which.

They had red buttons on their bright yellow jackets, flashing, with the words, "Have a Safe and Merry." Safe and merry what? Whoever made up the buttons ran out of room?

Just as they prepared to head inside and pull out Louis' unresponsive body, the sound stopped. The sudden silence made me dizzy. Mrs. Blackman clutched my arm.

We watched the doors to the hall. Several long seconds passed. Lonnie picked up his gear and turned to Brandon. "That's it. We're going in."

They surged forward just as the door opened, and Louis emerged, shaking his head. He seemed surprised at the official onlookers, but spoke directly to Mrs. Blackman, side-eying Thea and the responders. "Sorry it took so long. I had to rip out the wiring."

Mrs. Blackman patted his shoulder. "Can't be helped. I just don't understand how this young man was able to open the door. We keep it locked, always."

"I pulled the door tightly closed so maybe it's locked now." Louis allowed Brandon to look in his eyes with a light. "I didn't actually try it."

I pushed Colton towards Brandon. "This is the one that hit the switch, so he's been exposed, although he vacated the area quickly enough. Are you on the track team, Colton?"

Colton had the light shined in his eyes and was pronounced fit for duty. "What do you think that was?" Brandon asked his team mate. "About 90 decibels?"

"Sounds about right. Neither of you should have lasting damage. Your hearing will be back to normal in a few hours. See your doctor if you experience any ringing after two or three days." Lonnie was boss of the search and rescue team, a wee bit over-zealous in his ministrations perhaps, but competent. He'd rescued me from the bottom of a collapsed grave last year and, while I didn't need to be saved quite so enthusiastically, I was beyond grateful to get out of that hole. I'd spent over an hour with a 100-year-old skeleton, minus the skull.

"She went in after Colton," Reagan gestured at me. I didn't like the way she eyed my tote. "She's been yelling really loud."

Both responders pounced, and I slipped behind Mrs. Blackman's comforting bulk. They followed, and Lonnie squeezed my cheeks together and tilted my face up while Brandon used the light. "What are you looking for?" I mumbled through fish lips. Seemed to me those were the wrong orifices for the occasion.

Neither explained but declared I was good, and repeated the spiel they gave Louis and Colton. I was going to look this up online. I suspected the light was just a comforting gesture to make the subject believe they received a professional diagnosis. They loaded their bags into their yellow van and drove away, off to find another hapless victim to save before they had to take off their gear. "See you tomorrow night," I called after them.

SUGAR PLUM BLISS

I received a single flash of their emergency lights in return.

Mrs. Blackman thanked Louis effusively. I think she wanted to adopt him. He refused her offer of a cup of tea and Christmas cookies and edged toward his truck. I could have used a restorative cup of tea and a couple of cookies, but the formidable lady walked away after throwing me a dismissive glance. "Father Hanley will drop by the hall tomorrow evening to make sure you have everything you need."

Looking forward to that. If he did his spot check early enough, the party could be more or less respectable.

Thea rolled her eyes after Mrs. Blackman left. "We received a dozen noise complaints within five minutes. Not that we couldn't hear *The Twelve Days of Christmas* being played over and over ourselves. Neil asked me to respond unofficially. He thought you might have something to do with it. I'll tell him all is well and he can relax." She kicked her boots against the tires to knock off the snow and got into the scout.

"Remind Neil I'm not involved every time something goes wrong in this town," I called after her. Nervy of him.

Louis stood nearby, still shaking his head. "I saw your car in the lot and thought I'd stop by today and scope out the bar. It's portable and sometimes they move it."

"So, is it where you want it?" I asked.

"I didn't even notice. The noise was so bad, I ran straight to the media room, then straight back out after I pulled the wires. If the setup isn't suitable, I'll fix it tomorrow. I just want to go home now and take a nap. I have a shift at the Wing Nut tonight and it'll be busy."

"Right, of course. Thanks for helping, and see you tomorrow evening." Whoopee, he planned to show up!

I switched my attention to my assistants. Three of them looked moderately more alert than before the big noise; still not excited to be here. Colton pressed on his ears and released, over and over, like he was trying to squeeze a giant pimple out the top of his head. "Do you want to go home?" I asked him, raising my voice. This day wasn't getting any better.

"I'm good. My hearing is coming back. Still feels like my ears are filled with water, but it's getting better. I need to get these hours in."

"Luckily your exposure was short." Shorter than Louis'. How long does it take to pull a couple of wires? Foam ear plugs were scant protection from 90 decibels. Louis was either hero material, or an idiot.

I checked the time. "We have two hours and fifty minutes left, my precocious elves. Plenty of time to get the job done and make Mrs. Claus happy. Let's get in there and do this. Where's your Christmas cheer?" If I had pom-poms, I'd shake them.

They scowled at me, too cool to express cheer of any kind. Adrian and Marshall kicked snow around and threw a couple of snowballs at Reagan who rolled her eyes, then returned her scrutiny to my tote. A work stoppage loomed, although one needs to have started work in order to stop it.

"Okay, new deal," I told them. "Get the job done by four o'clock and I'll sign off on four hours each. And, please, help yourselves to the doughnuts. You eat and listen while I tell you what to do."

Deck the Halls – Finally

WHILE THE LITTLE TURKEYS gobbled up the doughnuts, I drew quick sketches for each wall, outlining where I wanted the garlands wrapped with white lights to be draped. "After you get them hung, I'll direct you in the placement of the ornaments." I knew better than to say the word 'balls' in a group of teenagers. "Everyone, please be careful of the nativity scene in the corner."

"Every piece is, like, five feet tall," Reagan said. "Kind of hard to miss."

She wasn't wrong. This was the biggest nativity scene in the world. Probably meant for outdoors. I should have asked Mrs. Blackman if she wanted us — meaning the kids — to move it to the front of the church. Nah, she knew where to find it.

Adrian and Marshall ventured away to find a ladder while Colton ate a third doughnut and helped me unbox garlands and lights. They returned with two ladders and we were on our way to magic land.

Reagan and Colton handed up lengths of garlands while Adrian and Marshall balanced on the top of the ladders and fixed them to the walls. They used a sticky product recommended — correction, make that demanded — by Mrs.

Blackman when I contacted her back in October about renting the hall and after I told her, yes, we were going to "swag" the garlands.

I thought it best to keep Colton off the ladders until his ears stopped ringing. Although, judging by the lip on him, he expected that swagging the garlands should be his job.

"Hey, Colton," I called to him. "Do you mind being the spotter? Step into the middle of the room every so often and make sure Adrian and Marshall swag the garlands evenly." Now that I knew 'swag' was a verb as well as a noun, I planned to use it a lot.

"I guess." He said it like spotting was a big imposition but I suspected he liked the added responsibility. The boy would go far in middle management.

Reagan handed up a plum ball to Marshall and wiped her brow like she'd spent a hot summer day on the road gang, in an orange jumpsuit. "Can I have my phone for a minute? I'll load my playlist. We'd at least have something to listen to other than Marshall farting on my head."

"It's the doughnuts. I'm super sensitive to white flour and ..."

"Absolutely not," I told her. "Breathe in the silence and think about all the new video games Santa is bringing you."

"I know exactly what my parents are getting me. It's on my list. I could play Christmas music. My Nana loves Bill Ivers and Buzz Croxly."

"Over my dead body, and I mean that in the most literal sense. And, I think you mean Burl Ives and Bing Crosby." How did I even know that?

When I planned the décor, I imagined three balls clustered together, one white and two plum, every two or three feet. These kids hung a random colour — whatever was handed up — wherever he felt like it. If I hadn't lost the will to live this morning in Canadian Tire, their haphazard efforts would finish me off.

"Good job," I encouraged. "You guys are nearly finished with the walls. Next, the Christmas tree. Remember, lights first, then graduate the size of ornaments. Smallest on top, largest on bottom. If you have any garland left, swag the bar. The room is looking awesome." It really wasn't but you get what you pay for.

My stomach rumbled, and I looked inside the doughnut box. They'd left me — not even a crumb.

All is Merry and Bright

THE KIDS SEEMED TO have the hang of things, so I decided they wouldn't miss me for a few minutes if I went to the kitchen and rifled through the cupboards and fridge for anything that wasn't past its best-by-due-date. I slung my tote over my shoulder in case Reagan noticed it was unattended and reached her sticky fingers inside for her phone.

The cupboards were bare of anything except crockery and glassware. The fridge ditto. Well, there was a sketchy container of something I preferred not to investigate. Nothing else in the kitchen other than the door to a utility room. Mops, a bucket, broom, the usual. I'd eat a jar of tomato sauce at this point but, alas, the room was devoid of edibles.

Neither Colton nor Louis had mentioned what the media room held other than a broken and, according to Colton, outdated, streaming system. At some dim time in history, it surely was a pantry. I hadn't eaten since breakfast. If the church ladies hid a stock of canned fruit, spaghetti, a box of cereal, anything, I'd embrace the Christmas spirit, cross my heart. I'd carry the empty can out in my tote and dispose of it in a dumpster. Of course, I'd replace it.

I stared at the doorknob of the media room, willing it to be unlocked and filled with cans of beans. This would be a great place to stash a secret hoard of sipping wine — for the priest during services. I sure wouldn't borrow that.

My hand rested on the knob. Hopeless, I was sure. Louis locked it. On the other hand, Mrs. Blackman asserted the door was already locked. What if the lock was simply defective, like the streaming equipment? What about that?

I turned the knob, pulled lightly, and the door flew open, the edge catching the tip of my left ear. I staggered back and caught the counter to keep my balance. What the ...? I felt my ear. No blood, but if it swelled, I might have to wear my hair down tomorrow night, not a good look for me when the humidity got at my curly mop.

My ears were taking a frightful beating today. When the pain subsided, I shoved off from the counter and bent to look at the lock. The bolt hadn't extended into the frame. It lay flat against the faceplate.

Surely Mrs. Blackman didn't carry a small key back and forth from the priest house. Bet the church ladies didn't each have a key to use every time one of them came in to set up or clean up from a funeral or other event. If I was a key, where would I be?

I found it in the first drawer to the left of the media room, all by itself. It was on a small keyring in the shape of — I'm guessing here — St. Francis, the one who liked animals since the figure held a lamb or rooster, hard to tell. I thought St. Francis had been demoted; but maybe that was St. Christopher.

No matter, the key fit the keyway perfectly. The bolt slid easily in and out of the lock mechanism with every turn of the key. Why didn't I just do the responsible thing and lock the door the way it should be?

I did a quick scan of the tiny room for food. Nope. However, on the floor lay a bag. A canvas carryall that looked like the one Louis had carried in, with tools to silence the noise from the streaming equipment. I thought back. I knew Louis carried a bag into the hall. I presumed he brought it out, but couldn't capture the image. Between ringing ears and a pounding head, I didn't remember.

I bent and unzipped the bag. Running my hands inside, I confirmed it was empty. For now, I'd assume it was a random bag. I closed the door and locked it, twisting the knob to ensure it was telling the truth this time. All secure.

A crash, followed by a string of curses erupted from the hall. I shoved the keyring back in the drawer and ran towards the swearing, my heart in my mouth. Did one of the kids fall? Mr. Archman said it was okay for them to stand on a stepladder.

A ladder was indeed on its side, but all four teens were upright and unhurt. I sank into a chair. "What happened?"

"Sorry, ma'am." Adrian set the ladder upright. "I jumped off the top rung and it flipped over."

"Almost knocked me flat." Colton glared at the other boy and shoved him.

Adrian shoved back, and I resisted the urge to roll my eyes. I stepped between them. "Okay, calm the ... calm down. We're almost done here."

They turned away from each other, muttering. What made me think these four were friends? They likely didn't run in the same pack at school, rather simply serving out their sentences. I had my own Breakfast Club here.

"Do you have anything for the top, Mrs. Redfern?" Reagan asked, examining the tree top critically.

They'd done an admirable job with the size placement of the balls. How long had I been out of the room? Guess the key thing took longer than I thought. I felt my left ear. Yep, swollen,

"You can call me Ms. Cornwall, or Bliss if you prefer. You'll find if you ever decide to get married that you'll prefer to retain your own identity."

"Yeah, my last name is Zerzinsky. Anything else would be an upgrade, especially if it starts with an A so I can be first for something instead of dead last all the time. I'll retain my identity another way."

"The world is in good hands with you, sister," I told her. And, yikes, I'd forgotten to buy a tree topper. I looked around before spotting the pile of plum Santa hats.

I ripped the tag off one and handed it to Reagan. "Will you do the honours?"

She looked from my face to the hat, then took it. The screeching sound from the ladder as she dragged it closer to the tree almost put me on my knees. My blood sugar was in the toilet, my head thumped and my left ear throbbed. Never mind, almost at the finish line.

Colton held the bottom of the ladder while Reagan positioned the hat at a jaunty angle. I clapped for her and, after a stunned silence, the boys followed suit. Reagan descended, trying her best to scowl.

Adrian fished around in the tree and, suddenly, the lights came on. If not magical, it was truly beautiful. "You had three battery powered light sets. We put two on the tree and the other on the bar. We needed some extension cords for the garlands on the wall and found a bunch in a wooden box in the coat room." He added, when I looked at him, "You know, the room to the left of the front doors where people leave their coats."

"We used up all the ornaments, so we flattened the boxes and put them in the recycling bin around back," Marshall offered.

How would we store them for next time? I made a concerted effort to speak. "Good thinking. Can we turn off the overhead lights?"

One of the kids hit the switch, and we were plunged into darkness. Except for the white lights on the 12-foot tree. A moment later, the room was bathed in a pale lavender glow as the garlands lit up. The random placement of the balls turned out fine, lovely in fact.

Marshall, looking much like a baby-faced vampire in the pale plum lighting, said, "I never thought of purple for Christmas before, but this is cool."

"Yeah, really cool," observed one of the other vampiric teens."

Reagan apparently concurred, "I love it." Chances were, her parents hadn't heard those words from her for a year or two.

I put my hands together in a namaste gesture and gave them a bow. "You guys rock. This is perfect. Thank you so much. Now, where are those forms?" The wall clock near the kitchen door showed 4:25 p.m. And they hadn't mentioned it.

I signed the forms and handed over their phones. When they slouched toward the front doors, I said, "Wait."

Thumbs already busy texting, they turned back. I held up a one-minute finger and scrabbled in my purse for my wallet. I realize we're a cashless society, but I always carried a small stash of the old stuff for when the bank machines go down. Hasn't happened to me yet, but I was ready.

I gave them each a twenty. They thanked me, all four of them, and none of them called me Mrs. Redfern. Best of all, I'd expense Glory for the money, under miscellaneous. Win-win.

Colton said, "Marshall and I only have two hours left for volunteer hours. If we get them in before the Christmas holidays, we can graduate in January. If you want, we'll come back on Sunday and take it all down for you. We'll even stay longer until it's done."

Marshall nodded. "Even if it takes three hours. We'll get extra forms from Mr. Archman on Monday and bring them to you to sign."

Reagan said, "I'll do the same."

"Me, too," vowed Adrian. "This was way more fun than most of my jobs."

I wanted to ask about the other jobs, but my stomach wouldn't let me. "That would be very helpful." I handed over a Bliss This House business cards to each of them. "Text me if you can't make it but, otherwise, I'll see you back here Sunday afternoon at two."

They insisted on giving me their phone numbers so I could text them with any change of plan. I locked the door after them and went back into the hall to look at the lighting. This could be very, very bad.

Oh, Christmas Lights, Keep Shining On

HOW COULD I FIX THIS? The plum pall filling the room would be super perfect for a Halloween party. Why didn't Chico warn me about the effects of tiny white lights against plum balls? This wasn't my fault — I never pretended to be an expert in party decorating, like a freaking wedding planner. I was rather incompetent, actually.

Mind you, we would need to turn on at least a few of the overhead pot lights, no matter what colour balls we used. Thankfully, they were dimmable. I experimented with the banks of lights and finally decided that leaving the outer two rows on dim showed the room to best advantage. I was quite relieved. The LED bulbs set to low sucked up most of the plum hue. I pulled my sleeve up and looked at my skin tone. Not bad at all. Christmas was saved.

I locked up and trudged through the slushy parking lot to my car. I picked up a handful of snow and pressed it against my hot ear. Ah, better. My phone buzzed and it took me a few minutes to fish it out of my purse. The church should really invest in extra lights out here.

Neil left six texts and called me twice. I'd heard noises from my purse but figured it was the other four phones blowing up. I called him back. "Yes, my darling husband. Are you home with my food?"

"Not yet. I'm just leaving the station. Where have you been all afternoon?"

"I'll tell you about it later. Food?"

"Again, any preference? Otherwise, don't complain."

"You could bring me a hot pepper enchilada on cheese-filled pizza crust and I'll still love you forever." Hunger brought out my sentimental side. I wasn't a fan.

"Okay, well, I'll be home in a half hour."

"I'll be waiting, sweet cheeks."

We lived ten minutes out of town. I made it in seven. By the time I heard Neil's Jeep in the driveway, I'd showered and eaten two hard-boiled eggs and a half dozen marshmallow Santas. Still starving.

Neil came in with our Black Lab, Bean, and two bags of food from the greasiest, saltiest franchise in town. "Yummy," I said. "What is it?"

"I got you a fish sandwich." He handed me one of the bags.

"Did you get me two? They're so little." I looked inside. Sadly, I was too hungry to really enjoy this. "And fries?"

"Yes to both. I'm always amazed at how much a small person can eat."

"Amazing there's still mystery in our relationship. What did you get?"

He immediately looked guilty and pretended he hadn't heard me.

I finished swallowing before I spoke. "You got yourself a double cheeseburger with two big slabs of mystery meat, didn't you?"

"Maybe."

I looked at his bag. There was more stuff packed in there than in mine. "You got two. And double fries."

"How's your sandwich made from a two-headed fish caught in a sludge lake in the oil fields? I can go eat in the office if you'd rather." Getting huffy, now.

"No, carry on. There's an upside for me if you keel over before you're forty."

"That gives me seven years. What's the upside?"

"Big life insurance policy. Health benefits for life. Fully paid-off mortgage. Investments all to myself. Yeah, party time for Bliss Moonbeam Cornwall. Don't worry, though. If you're merely incapacitated, I'll make sure to place you in a nice facility where you can sit and watch TV all day. I'll be young enough to find a hot new boyfriend, maybe an OPP officer since I'm used to guns. Or, a firefighter."

He put three fries in his mouth. "Sounds like we have a plan. What kind of day did you have, anyway?"

Usually I like it when he stands up to me, but romance was off the table tonight. I tried to tell him about my day, but he constantly interrupted me by answering his phone and going into the hall to talk. Then, he'd call someone else while he was out there. I couldn't make out a word.

When he came back, he said, "So, you ran over Chico and some other guy with your shopping cart. What happened next?"

"I did not ... Who were you just talking to?"

"Work-related. I can't discuss it just yet. Go ahead, I'm listening. What happened to your ear, by the way? It looks inflamed."

"You're going to the party tomorrow night. Don't conjure up some emergency. Your team can handle it on their own."

"I'll be there. Wouldn't miss it."

His phone rang again, and I gave up. All the fat I just consumed sent me into a burp-fest which turned into hiccups. I drank some ginger ale and went to bed.

I was just drifting off when a thought struck me and I sat straight up. The sugar plums. I forgot to pick up the sugar plums from the bakery.

Sugar Treats and Festive Nails

AS SOON AS THE SWEET Shoppe Bakery opened at eight o'clock the next morning, I picked up my 20 dozen assorted cookies, Nanaimo bars, and other desserts, as well as 14 dozen sugar plums, to coordinate with the plum décor.

When I first approached them, the bakery didn't know how to make sugar plums the traditional way. I mean, that's why the internet was invented, but I researched a suitable recipe myself, shopped in three different stores for the ingredients and lugged them to the bakery. No way was I going to spend free time I didn't have in the kitchen making a million two-inch balls.

The owner of the bakery called me in a few days ago for a taste test. Wow, they weren't bad at all. I ate six right there. Only one problem. The balls were rolled in sugar. White sugar. That wasn't the look I wanted. Back to the bulk store for a sack of plum-dyed sugar. I accepted their word the dye they used was food-grade.

I tried a couple more in the bakery to make sure the purple sugar made the cut. Nothing wrong here, and I handed over the town credit card once more. Glory would have a screech-fit when she saw the expenses I'd racked up for this hoedown. Before Christmas next year, I planned to dump her and focus on my own businesses.

It took me six trips to transport the 34 boxes to my trunk a half block away. Not a single sugar plum was harmed, except the two I ate after the last box was loaded.

Next, I picked up Neil's dress pants at the cleaners. He wanted to go into town himself but I couldn't get behind that option, instead encouraging him to clean the eavestroughs again or take a nap. Anything, just stay away from the station. If something was going down, he didn't need to take part. He had people for that. According to my information chain, composed of women who worked for me or who I came in contact with during my official duties, nothing major in the criminal department was happening in Lockport.

I skidded into my manicure appointment with two minutes to spare. Winnie, also the owner of Twinkle Nails, liked her clients to be early, even if they sat and waited while she finished up with someone else. The usual soothing spa music filled the room, decorated only with a big screen TV hanging on one wall. The screen morphed slowly through photos of faraway rainforests and pyramids, or deserts of shifting sand. No humans or beasts. I relaxed for the first time in days.

Until the woman a few stations over insisted, loudly, that her nail technician free-paint Christmas scenes on her nails. "No stencils," she said. "I want to look natural. Nothing fake. Please."

Winnie shut down the electric sander-type thing she was using to remove the old shellac from my nails. She spoke to the woman, "We are not graphic artists in here. If we were, we'd make more money working for a comic book franchise. You'll have stencils or nothing."

The other technician sent Winnie a grateful smile, and the blonde woman's pale complexion flushed. "Sorry. Can I see your stencils? Please."

I knew that voice. I craned my neck to get a better look. It took me a minute to place her, the way it does when you meet someone outside their usual habitat.

Winnie gave my hand a shake. "You. Have you decided what colour you want?"

"Yes. I'll go with the neutral light pink, the matte." I read out the number from her colour chart. My choice had a faint lavender tone I hoped would complement the lighting at the church hall, not make me look like I had newly risen from a grave.

"Good call. You'll have a rhinestone on each thumb for the party."

Since it was not exactly a request, I nodded. While she set to work with the colour, tapping my hand impatiently when it was time to stick my fingers into the UV dryer, I spoke to the woman beside me.

"Piper, right? You work at the Wing Nut."

She gave me a considered look. "Of course. I've seen you there with the big, blond guy, usually Friday nights for dinner. He's the police chief. Your boyfriend?"

"Used to be. Husband now."

She looked me over. "Lucky you. Bet he's hot in bed."

After a moment's silence, I said, "You know it," and introduced myself. "Bliss Cornwall. Nice to meet you outside the bar. You must know Louis pretty well. He's bartending for the First Responders' Gala tomorrow night at St. Mary's."

"Louis and I are a couple. We both started at the Wing Nut at the same time about six months ago. We'll probably move on by spring. We don't like to stay in one place for long. So much to see, so little time, you know how it is."

"Sure. Do you and Louis always work in bars?"

"That's where the money is, hon. In tips, not so much the pay."

Her formidable chest didn't seem as intimidating in an oversized hoodie. The low-cut tops she wore at work likely earned her larger tips than, say, someone like me if I worked there.

Winnie tapped my right hand. "Change."

I gave her my left hand to work on, wondering if I should mention the empty canvas bag in the media room at St. Mary's to Piper. Pretty sure it was Louis', but he'd be at the hall tonight and could pick it up himself.

Conversation fizzled out and for a few minutes, I enjoyed the tranquility of the salon. When Winnie finished with me, she escorted me to the register where I paid with my debit card and gave her the small gift I'd picked up at the chocolate shop down the street — a box of the raspberry truffles I knew she favoured.

"See you at the Wing Nut, Piper," I called out as I left.

She raised a hand, the fingertips colourful with stenciled gingerbread men and reindeer with red noses. "If not before. Catcha later, babe."

SUGAR PLUM BLISS

I drove to St. Mary's and hauled in the pastry boxes, letting myself in with the keys Mrs. Blackman loaned me. *I expect these returned to the drop box outside the church office by 5 p.m. on Sunday, Mrs. Redfern. No exceptions.* Unless she was sitting in the shrubbery with a glass of eggnog, timing me, how would she know I didn't leave the keys at, say 5:06 p.m.? It would be just like me to try that.

Since I was in the hall kitchen anyway, I tried the door to the media room. If the thing opened, I'd have to believe in evil Christmas elves, or Krampus.

It didn't budge. I gave it an approving pat and checked the first drawer to the left. The St. Francis keyring lay where I'd found it. If, for some otherworldly reason, the damaged system stirred to life and blasted out *The Twelve Days of Christmas* at 90 decibels during the gala, I could tell someone else where to find the keys. There'd be plenty of first responders on the scene.

On my way out, I plugged in the garland lights, and the two outer rows of pot lights, dimming them. Not perfect, but not so Halloween-y that guests should snicker behind my back for years to come.

Last chore of the day. I stopped at Glory's Tudor-style mansion in the Arlington Woods neighbourhood. Pan, Glory's housekeeper, answered the door and I stepped into the spacious entrance with the sweeping staircase to the upper floor.

I gave him the church hall keys. He promised to be at the hall at 5 p.m. to bump up the heat, and whatever else needed doing. I'd been elated to learn Pan had worked for a wedding consultant in Vancouver before he landed in Lockport. He'd had many occasions to regret letting slip that part of his past.

"What exactly do you want me to do, again?" he asked. "The Lady and her Lord are still in her boudoir, but should be up soon."

"Still in bed? They should get married. That would end the honeymoon phase. I want you to ... you know ... get the hall into a festive mood, tables set around the dance floor. You'll find linens somewhere. The bartender, Louis something, will show up around that time to set up the bar. A couple of my Bliss This House staff will get the oven going for hot appetizers. They'll act as servers. You instruct them when and where as they aren't professional wait staff. Can you do all that?"

"Sure. Why am I doing this, again?"

Hearing voices on the second floor, I backed out of the entrance doors. "Because it will get you out of a few hours of waiting on the Frost Empress and her consort."

"Right. Merry Christmas to me."

Tis the Season to be Purple

NEIL CARRIED ME FROM the Jeep to the front steps of the church hall. No way was I hiking through two inches of snow in my Oscar de la Renta ankle bootees. They were suede leather with cut-out cuffs and three-inch heels, far too precious to be exposed to the December elements.

He didn't complain. I think he hoped a few of the firemen in attendance would see him hoisting his wife across the parking lot. Neil thought a couple of them had a crush on me, which could have been true. I'm pretty cute, so it happens. In any case, Neil weighs 100 pounds more than I do, and spends three hours a week at the gym, so carrying me a few hundred yards wasn't going to kill him even if no one saw him do it.

The outside of the hall looked festive enough with the two cedar trees on either side of the entrance lit with white twinkle lights. The church had to be responsible for that. In the foyer, we hung our coats on a rack, and I estimated about 20 guests had already arrived.

As coordinator of this party, I should have arrived well before any of the guests, but it took me far too long to coax Neil into his black dress pants, black shirt, and charcoal jacket. He complained every step of the way, insisting he looked like an Italian mob boss. I assured him the dark tones made his blond hair pop and the plum tie added just the right touch of seasonal colour to his outfit. That left me with only two hours to take a nap and get ready.

Neil waited while I re-applied my lip gloss and straightened my dress over my hips. The ankle boot heels raised me to a satisfactory five feet five, still nine inches shorter than Neil but at least my head skimmed his shoulder. He would dance with me tonight if it killed him.

"Why is that dress so short?" he asked. "Don't bend over or you'll give the party a floorshow they won't soon forget. They'll be able to see the Yukon."

I ignored him and poked at my up-do until it was centred firmly in place again. Neil stuck his head into the party room, pulled it back out and said, "You didn't tell me the decorations were going to be purple. I thought you wanted my tie to match your dress."

"My dress is plum," I told him. "So is your tie. I spent more than four hours with a crew of cranky teenagers to get this hall decorated, and I thought it would be lovely for the two of us to match the décor."

"You can match," he replied, taking off his tie and shoving it into the pocket of his sport jacket. "I'll go for the casual look. Since when are Christmas decorations purple?"

"Plum," I corrected him once again, but I guessed not for the last time. "There are white accents, if you look closely."

"I like red and green. Let's go in and get this over with."

Glory Yates, Royal Empress of Lockport, initially decided the party would be for town council members and their spouses only. When I pointed out that would mean about 12 people were eligible and we may as well hold the party at her house, she surrendered, and the hall was filling up with not only council members, but firefighters, cops, city works personnel, and paramedics and their partners. A few dozen guests swarmed through the room, mingling, drinking, and eating appetizers. More entered the building behind us, stamping the snow from their shoes in the foyer, stopping off at the coat room.

As we stepped across the threshold, a deafening bang sounded close to my ear.

"Holy shit," I yelled. Didn't my ears suffer enough yesterday? Neil's right hand reached for his hip where his gun usually rested in its leather holster.

Pan stood beside a four-foot, brass gong with a wooden mallet in his hand. He waited until the vibration stopped before calling out, "Police Chief Neil Redfern and his wife, Bliss Moonbeam Cornwall-Redfern."

Neil gave Pan a hard look. "What's that for?"

"It wasn't my idea," Pan said. "Her Gloryness told me to announce everyone who comes in. I don't even know most of these people by name. I have to ask them first. Sorry."

The crowd laughed. Obviously, this was funny as long as it wasn't happening to you. And, indeed it was. The next couple who came in was hilarious. The lady dropped her purse and, when her companion reached down to retrieve it, his ass hit the gong, and we all had a second good laugh. Except Neil. He headed for the bar. He hated social events of any kind, especially the kind that forced him to put on dress pants and jacket. In his view, wearing a uniform five days a week meant he should be able to wear jeans and tee shirts on the weekends.

I was used to seeing most of these people in uniforms, so had to take a second look before identifying them. When a tall man nudged my shoulder to get my attention, I wound up to punch him back, then recognized my old high school buddy, Fang Davidson. He was one of five volunteer firemen who augmented the full-timers. At first, Glory wasn't going to let the volunteers attend her *la-di-da* party but I told her I'd heard talk of a wildcat strike in support of those left out of the seasonal festivities. I lied, but she didn't know what a wildcat strike was, so caved once again and invited not only the volunteer firefighters, but the animal control and by-law officers.

"Fang, is that really you? Why did you shave your beard? I've never seen you without one, even in high school. My world just shifted."

"It scared little Bentley, for some reason. The others were okay with it." He stroked his chin that was a half shade lighter than the rest of his face, not having been exposed to daylight in over 15 years.

Fang and his wife recently added a sixth child to their family. Since his wife was a nurse, it had to be on purpose. "Where is Leanne?" The poor woman could use a night out.

"Harley has a virus, and Leanne wanted to stay with her. Looks like some of the other kids are coming down with the same thing." Think about that for a minute. Fang and Leanne had a daughter, full name Harley Davidson.

I took a few steps away from Fang in case he coughed on me. As well as a Harley, he had an Edsel and a Packard, genders unknown to me, and I couldn't remember the names of the others, but they were along the same automotive lines. I just hoped the kids learned to fight before kindergarten.

"Nice purple dress," Fang commented, and took a slurp of his beer. "You match the decorations. Where did you get so much of the same colour?"

The gong rang out and we stopped to laugh with the rest of the room.

"We all need a change from the boring green and red tradition. I had to work with the tight budget Her Cheapness the Mayor allotted me. Looks good, though, right?" I glanced down at my Oscars and rubbed the right toe against Fang's pants. I thought there was a smudge, but it turned out to be a shadow.

He jumped back. "What's wrong with you? You're lucky Leanne isn't here. Your husband is, though, so watch it. I don't need a run-in with him. Can't you convince him we weren't an item in high school? He always looks at me like he wants to drag me into an alley and kick the shit out of me."

"Don't be paranoid. He'd never do such a thing. He'd send one of his guys. A few of the older cops remember the Halloween you tipped the porta-potties over in the park and dragged them behind the bleachers at the soccer field, leaking every inch of the way."

"That was 15 years ago, and you were there, too. Anyway, I'm only at this shindig because I told Chico I'd help him set up his photography station." Fang opened his jacket to show me a glass bottle sticking up from the inside pocket. "Later, if you get bored, you, me and Chico can hunker down under the food table and drink tequila like we did back in the day. Just don't let your husband see you."

"Ah, taking a hard pass on that one. I'm the designated driver tonight so, even if I could stand the smell of tequila after senior year, I must let my handsome, blond god of love drink more than one beer. Which means nothing for me."

I closed in on Pan, and ripped the wooden mallet out of his hand. "Where are Glory and Tony? This is her party."

Pan peered around me at the entrance to the cloak room, waiting for another unsuspecting couple to announce. "They should be here any minute. I did everything you asked, even helped set up the bar, and directed the table placement for the catering staff. I can't hear properly because of the stupid gong."

"Sucks to be you." I handed back the mallet. "I spent yesterday afternoon in here decorating with teenagers. Don't cry to me."

"It's all very purple ... He took a look at my face and added, "But atmospheric. I love all the white lights wound through the garlands and balls."

Neil strode up to us and warned Pan with a look not to use the mallet. Pan melted behind the gong while Neil used his outside voice to get the room's attention.

"Just one public safety announcement," he said, to accompanying jeers and boos, mostly from the firefighters. Neil's lips twitched in an almost-smile. Whatever he had to say, he was loving it. He dodged a balled-up napkin.

"One of my on-duty officers has set up a breathalyzer station by the exit."

I joined Pan behind the gong.

SUGAR PLUM BLISS

"I'm sure we all want to arrive home safely. Therefore, any individuals who register any level of alcohol will please deposit their vehicle keys with the officer. A bus will be waiting in the parking lot at midnight for those who don't live within walking distance. The bus ride is compliments of the Town of Lockport. You can pick up your keys tomorrow at the police station. If you don't wish to try out our new breathalyzer, deposit your keys anyway. Thank you, and enjoy your evening."

I poked my head around the gong. So many mouths were open, there was a moment's silence. Then, the room erupted in arguments, mostly between spouses about which one couldn't have a drink. For some, it was too late. Neil and I should have arrived sooner to hand out flyers at the door.

I slapped Pan on the back and yanked on his stubby, black ponytail. "O-M-G, I'm dying. This is the best Christmas party I've been to, yet." I dragged him into the open. "Here's your mallet. Gong away. I'm going to the bar."

That's the Spirit!

"HEY, BLISS. WHAT CAN I get you?" Louis swiped the granite bar counter with a wet cloth I trusted was clean, and fingered his bolero tie.

A glass bowl sat atop the bar, containing a few loonies and one toonie. I hoped the big tips I promised him were forthcoming. You'd think a church hall wouldn't have a bar, but you would be oh so wrong. St. Mary Immaculate had a lovely one, but the priest was smart enough not to keep liquor on the premises. Whoever rented the room had to bring their own. The liquor license for this affair was duct-taped to the wall behind the bar, but I didn't examine it too closely. It was possible that Louis printed off the license and signed it himself, and I wanted to be able to plead ignorance with a clear conscience if Neil noticed.

"I want a tall glass with ice, filled with half water, and the other half a combo of orange juice and cranberry juice. Sugar-free, please."

"Want gin in that? Maybe vodka?" Louis slipped a 12-ounce flute from under the bar and poured ice in.

"Just straight, thanks."

When my peachy-coloured drink was ready, he said, "That'll be seven dollars even."

I almost choked on the first sip. "What? Seven dollars for watery juice and ice cubes? That's not right."

"I'm charging the same as we do at the Wing Nut. This is their liquor and their juice. I can't do anything about the prices."

Crap. I could've had nine ounces of wine for that price. I reached for Louis' tie, just to straighten it, when the back of my dress was yanked down.

"I told you not to bend over," Neil whispered in my ear.

"My dress isn't that short. Anyway, my underwear is the same colour. Plum."

He briefly closed his eyes, then addressed Louis. "What's the fuss, here?"

Louis grabbed his cloth and swirled it over the bar, avoiding Neil's question.

"He's charging me seven dollars for a glass of juice, mostly water and ice." I threw Louis a smug look. He was gonna get it now.

Neil placed a couple of bills on the bar. "Give her all the juice she wants. If you need more money, come and find me."

Good one. Like Louis would chase after the police chief and ask for juice money. If I had to spend half the night in the ladies' room, I vowed to keep drinking.

The Ice Queen
Cometh

BY THE TIME I TURNED around with my drink, Neil had disappeared. He probably sensed I wanted to dance with him. The only time we'd danced was at our wedding. He was quite competent but disliked it. I always figured it was because I was short and, in my regular two-inch heels, my nose hit his nipple level. We probably looked ridiculous. Tonight, though, my Oscars would raise me enough for him to bend and nuzzle my neck with his warm, firm lips. In public? As if, hah. Whatever, he was going to dance with me or I'd ... maybe dance with a fireman.

In hot pursuit of my police chief, or the fire chief, whichever I found first, the house lights came up fully, turning the guests purple. Everyone looked around in confusion, but it turned out that Pan was excitedly waving his mallet near the gong. Must be a VIP arriving.

Wait! I leaped for the light switches and turned off the pot lights except for the outer two rows.

The only VIP — in her own mind — was Glory. I expected a ringing worthy of a queen and her prince, but Pan must've been warned beforehand. He barely touched the gong with the mallet.

"Presenting, Her Honour the Mayor of Lockport, Glory Yates, and her escort, Ontario Provincial Police Detective-Sergeant, Anthony Pinato."

Someone tugged at my dress and I knew without turning it was Neil. I was going to deck that man if he kept trying to lengthen my hem. I mean, the fabric didn't stretch vertically. What didn't he get about that?

"Now, that's a dress," Neil commented, earning him another demerit for noticing Glory's apparel.

Gotta say, though, it was spectacular. Oodles more fabric than mine, in a waterfall of shimmery folds that changed colour with every movement, like angel's wings. The bitch. If I'd known she'd wear a Bronx and Banco design, I'd have picked something else. Neil was right. My purple piece of crap was too short, and my Oscar bootees couldn't make up for the dress's shortcomings.

Chico followed Glory and Tony around like they were celebrities, taking shots from every angle with his Nikon and telescopic lens. What was he trying to photograph? Her nose hairs? She wore a short, faux fur white cape over the dress and she handed it to Tony to hold so Chico could take a few shots of her tossing her red-gold hair over her shoulder, giving the crowd a good look at her bare, flawless back.

I'd warned Chico not to take unflattering photos of anyone tonight, especially me. He didn't need to go overboard with the glamour shots. I gave the back of my dress a tug. Fang and Chico had set up a backdrop corner covered with green garlands, plum balls, and white fairy lights. Where'd they get the extra decorations? Subjects were going to look really plum in their official photo unless Chico did some magic with his lighting. And, too bad for the women who wore a dress that clashed, like red or green. The men should be fine.

Getting Into the
Christmas Spirit

I NEEDED A REFILL AND headed for the bar. On the way, I dodged the revellers who had discovered the buffet tables and converged like an infestation of starving cockroaches.

"Hit me again, Louis," I said plunking my glass on the bar. "This time, a little more water, please." Both oranges and cranberries were high-acidic and, already, my stomach was rebelling. Better get some food down there for the acid to work on.

"How about carbonated water this time?" he asked. "It gives the juice some pizzazz. Makes you burp, though."

"A good burp is always therapeutic. Fizzy water it is."

Louis rustled up my heart-burn special. "Why can't you drink? I heard the announcement about the bus. Why do you have to drive your husband home? He hasn't even come back for a second beer."

"He gets carsick in a bus," I said "Don't tell him I said that." Really, I had no idea why Neil wouldn't ride the bus.

I turned the questions back on Louis. "Do you know you forgot your canvas bag in the media room yesterday? With all that noise, you probably thought you locked the door by pulling it closed, right? Not to worry, though, I found the key and locked it up for you. I'll open it for you later."

"I remembered when I got home. My ears were ringing so bad, I forgot it. I couldn't find a pair of snips in the bag to cut the wires so I had to rip them out of the wall. Just wanted to get out of there."

Yeah, hard to find a tool in an empty bag, but I didn't say that out loud. Something weird about this bag thing ...

Chico and Fang joined me, one on either side. Both ordered beers, so predictable, so boring. What is it about men and beer? Would it kill them to order a glass of wine once in a while?

"Listen, Bliss," Chico said, with a covert glance over his shoulder. "Neil is talking to Glory and her man-toy. Now's a good time to slip under the table and drink Fang's bottle of tequila. For old time's sake."

"Can't this time around, guys. I'm in charge of this festival of jollity." Even though it seemed to be rolling along fine without my direct supervision at the moment.

I decided to check out the food, then turned back. "Chico, there are people lining up to have their photos taken. Fang, you can help him by keeping order in the line. Things can take a sudden turn for the ugly when firefighters and cops are in the same room drinking beer."

"Yes, boss," Chico replied, saluting me with his bottle. Not even a glass. So barbaric.

"Oh, and Chico? You might not want to repeat that man-toy remark in Glory's hearing, or she'll turn you into a pillar of ice."

Before he wandered away in Chico's wake, Fang leaned over. "I don't want to alarm you, but your dress is so short, I caught a glimpse of your panties. Just a heads-up."

"You wish," I told him, jabbing him in the stomach with my elbow.

I made a side trip to the kitchen to check on my cleaning staff-turned-caterers. Appetizers rotated in and out of the oven with satisfactory efficiency. I checked the refrigerated unit to make sure the desserts were ready, including the special sugar plums as well as the usual seasonal cookies and cheesecake selections.

A door to the side alley of the church thumped softly. For the moment, I was alone in the kitchen. "Hello?" I called. "Who is it?" I'm not stupid enough to answer a knock on a door, church or not, without knowing who was on the other side.

No one answered. I pressed my ear to the door and heard light footsteps running towards the sidewalk at the front of the church. I opened the door and looked left in time to see a figure turn the corner and disappear. I felt bad. Maybe that was someone who needed help. So close to Christmas, too. In that case, they should have identified themselves and asked for Father Who's-it who owned the church. Ran the church, I meant.

In the party room, the gong was silent. Pan and the mallet were missing from their post. Everyone who planned to show up, had. I spotted Pan circling the groups of guests with platters of food, his short frame dwarfed by the bulked-up firefighters and cops. The two bylaw enforcement officers weren't bad, either.

Fruitcakes, We Got Plenty

I HAD A WORD WITH THE DJ, telling him if he played one more Christmas Carol in the next hour, I'd dock his pay. Soon, the yowling notes of a band unknown to anyone over 30 caused a few people to drop their food. I went back and told Mr. Smart-Ass DJ what the next selection better be.

I stopped to admire the 12-foot Scotch pine that stood in the middle of the room (odd place for it, but I didn't put it there). The tree dazzled the eye.

Unfortunately, someone had again turned on more overhead pot lights than the two outer rows. An eerie glow settled over the entire room, including the guests. I kept my back turned to Chico. I felt his eyes burning a hole in the back of my head. He would undoubtedly complain of the filters he had to apply so his photography subjects didn't look like they were guests at a vampire wedding. I turned off the extra lights and the room returned to its former lavender tint.

I rounded the tree and found my husband sitting at a café-height table with Glory and Tony. I climbed onto the fourth chair and looked around. Nobody was drinking; they all looked glum.

"Hi, there. I don't see much Christmas spirit happening here. The Chief of Police and the Mayor with her handsome consort should be out there mingling."

Neil wasn't a social animal, as I believe I've mentioned. Tony was more fun at a party, but Glory had been mopey for weeks, and Tony wouldn't leave her side. This wouldn't do.

Just then, the DJ remembered who was paying him and launched into Anne Murray's, *Could I Have This Dance.* "We're dancing to this," I said to Neil, and yanked on his arm until he slowly stood up like I asked him to re-shingle the roof in mid-February when his favourite hockey team was playing. That would be the Leafs but, oh well.

He soon got into the mood, although we stayed in the shadows. I put my arms around his neck. He moved them to his waist and uttered one word. "Dress."

Whatever. My Oscars gave me the extra inches to rest my face against his chest. His hands drifted downwards, then up to squeeze my shoulders and draw me in closer. I lifted my face. I reached around his waist to give his excellent butt a pat. "Hey, why did you wear your gun, for crap's sake? This is a party."

"I just feel naked without it," he replied, looking over my shoulder towards the kitchen area.

I was hungry. About time they rolled out the desserts. "Speaking of naked. On the way home, I know a nice, abandoned cemetery we can stop at for a few minutes. I promise your engine won't even cool down."

He bent and kissed me. It was a long, good one. "I don't see why not. It's been a while since we made out in a cemetery."

"It was our wedding night. I remember." That was almost four months ago. Good times.

When the song ended, he pulled my dress down one more time and went back to his table, trying to herd me with him. I escaped and cruised the room, looking for troublemakers. Finding the crowd well enough behaved, I picked up a crab appetizer and wandered over to the nativity scene beside the now-silent gong. The camel was five feet high with the other figures not much shorter. All of them except the baby in the manger wore plum Santa hats. One hat topped the tree; I'd wondered where the rest had disappeared to. This departing gesture by my decorating team was very rude, but the very thing I'd planned to do with the hats.

The animals, especially the goat, looked quite festive with the white pompom hanging in front of their faces. Wait! I took another look. Goat? Shouldn't that be a sheep? Perhaps a pagan had slipped in the symbol of Satan as a joke. Who cared. It was great.

At the photo setup. Chico and Fang had their heads together in serious discussion. I wheeled around, not wanting to get pulled into whatever mischief they were planning. I didn't disappear fast enough.

"Hey, Bliss, come here." Chico reached out and clutched my arm. "I have an idea."

"Probably not a good one." I tried to edge away, but Fang had my other arm.

"No, really. You'll like it. Totally harmless." Chico laid out his idea and it honestly sounded like fun. Liven up this tedious party.

"Okay, but wait a minute. I need to do something first. You get set up." I ran back to the table and rifled through Neil's jacket pockets until I found my tiny mirror and lip gloss. None of the three so much as looked over at me. My nose was a little shiny, but I hadn't brought anything for that. Grabbing a napkin off the table, I pressed it over my nose to soak up the oil. There, totally cute again.

Back with the guys, I said, "Okay, how do you want to do this?"

They had dragged two ornate chairs into the make-shift photo booth. By the side of each chair, they placed a four-foot wise man, their plum Santa hats sitting rakishly on their heads. Nice touch.

Chico fiddled with the Nikon for a while longer, then he and Fang sat down on the chairs. "I've set the timer to go off every six seconds for two minutes."

"So, where am I going to sit?"

They patted their knees.

"Uh, no. Do you want Neil to freak out? You know he thinks I was involved with you in high school," I said to Fang. "He isn't sure how you," I poked Chico on the shoulder, "fit in."

"We aren't doing anything but having a bit of fun. Our wives aren't here and this party is dying on its feet," Fang said.

Both of them had a few drinks down the hatch already, or they wouldn't be so cavalier about Neil. Usually, they were scared to look at me in public. On the other hand, if my husband chose to ignore me in a social setting, he shouldn't complain that I found innocent fun elsewhere.

Chico handed me a plum Santa hat and one to Fang, plunking another on his own head. At this rate, the entire nativity scene would be without head warmers. The hat was big on me, and only my ears prevented it from falling over my eyes.

My left ear had healed quite well overnight and hardly twinged, although I feared for my up-do. But, what the hey, no one was paying attention to me anyway.

The guys had glasses of tequila, while I held the half-empty bottle. For two minutes, we posed and postured for the camera, making silly faces. Just before the two-minute beeper sounded, I lay across their knees and held the bottle aloft, kicking one Oscar-shod foot into the air. This might make a good holiday photo for the December newsletter for my Bliss This House staff.

Laughing our asses off, we looked up to see a throng of interested onlookers surrounding us. "Can you do some for us?" the fire chief's wife asked. I think her name was Jill. "That looks like more fun than the formal photo."

Always the businessman, Chico said, "Sure, just take a seat and let me reset the camera. I'll download the photos in the next few days and send them on to you, if you don't mind writing your email on this list."

I watched for a few minutes, while the couples lined up to take their turn at groping their partner or hoisting glasses into the air. Most of the men had taken off their jackets and rolled up their sleeves. A lot of muscles were on display. Could partial nudity be far behind? I looked around for Neil, but he was nowhere in sight.

I left the photo shoot, returning to the table. No Neil, and it seemed Glory and Tony hadn't moved from their chairs. Something was definitely wrong.

"Glory, you should take the mic and say a few words, as mayor and official host of this bizarre event." She hadn't lifted a gilt-lacquered fingernail, but that's why I got paid the big bucks

— to do the work and give her the credit. "Because of the bus, everyone in the room is ushering in the holiday season with a lot of spirits."

"I will, Bliss. In due time." Glory didn't meet my eyes, just stroked the back of Tony's hand. Could she be planning to fire me? This would be the best Christmas ever.

"Be right back," I told them. At the buffet table, I filled a tray with appetizers and desserts. The servers hadn't brought out the sugar plums yet. I'd get them out of the fridge as soon as I dropped off this load with Glory and Tony.

I stopped in my tracks just out of sight around the tree when I heard their low voices. Sounded serious and I didn't want to interrupt. I shoved a bacon and cheese tidbit into my mouth and looked around for Neil. Where the hell was he? A couple of guests passed me and took an appetizer off the tray. Hey!

"Get your own food, people. This is mine." With the DJ blasting the freaking chipmunk Christmas song, I don't think they heard me. Tony and Glory sat inches from me and I heard their voices, not clearly, but enough to know I shouldn't be listening.

"I don't think I can bear it." Glory whispered the words.

"We'll get through it together, if it turns out ... bad." Tony had taken a knife wound to the throat a few years back, and his voice was hoarse at the best of times. Now, emotion caused his words to fade out.

I backed up and left them to their serious discussion. Whatever it was about, it was the source of Glory's agitation and sadness the past while. She hadn't screamed at me for weeks, and that was scary.

It Ain't Father Christmas

MY TRAY BUMPED THE back of a man dressed in a long, black dress. Make that a cassock. Mrs. Blackman told me his name, but now I blanked.

He turned around and aimed an intimidating set of white eyebrows at me. After one quick glance at my legs displayed in all their natural glory, he refastened his glare on my face. His frown indicated the sight wasn't much more to his liking.

"Have an appetizer, Father ... um, ah ..." I thrust the tray towards him and glanced around for a Catholic who might know the priest's name. When I looked back at him, he was staring over my shoulder at the nativity scene, some figures still sporting plum Santa hats. Then, he focussed on the photography setup where couples cavorted minus shoes, jackets, but luckily with pants and dresses still intact although a few of the guests waiting their turns appeared to be wrestling with zippers and buttons. Geez, I'd been to cop parties before and things could get ugly but the spouses or partners stayed sober. I was beginning to think that Neil's bus idea wasn't a very smart one. Most of the guests obviously opted for that choice, so no checks on the drinking.

Nobody paid attention to the priest. Surely, some of them were part of the guy's flock. Desperate to move his attention away from the debauchery to something more calming to his nerves, I grabbed his arm, only later thinking it wasn't right to manhandle a priest. "Come with me, Father. How about some food?" I pushed my tray into his hands.

I remembered hearing that priests like to drink. I hauled him towards the bar. "How about a nice glass of wine? Or, whisky." Yes, priests liked whisky. You see that on TV all the time.

The tray clattered to the bar top. He caught Louis' eye. "I'll have a Glenlivet. On the rocks."

"Sorry, Padre, don't have that here. This is a bullet and fire show. They don't pay for expensive whisky." Louis reached under the bar and placed two bottles on the counter. "I can give you either Jameson Black Barrel or Johnny Walker."

The priest scowled at the bottles, then said, "Give me the Jameson, double, on the rocks. And, the name is Father Hanley."

Great, I had his name now. Glass in hand, Father Hanley walked away from me. Louis and I stared at each other.

"That'll be 17 dollars, Bliss."

"How much is left from what my husband gave you?"

"Six dollars."

He was lying. "As you can see, I'm not carrying a purse. I'll send Neil over to speak to you." As soon as I found him.

I left the tray of cold appetizers on the bar top for Louis and headed for the kitchen. There was a microwave here if he wanted to heat them up. Time to bring out the sugar plums. I pulled one of the four trays from the fridge and set it on a nearby counter. I was retrieving a second tray when I heard a rap on the door to the alley. Not wanting to turn a needy person away a second time, I opened the door.

Bad Tidings

THE WOMAN STANDING in the alley didn't look homeless or hungry. I looked her over. Warm padded coat, red Canadiens toque, hands in pockets. We locked eyes for an instant before she glanced over my shoulder. The toque covered her blonde hair, but I recognized her. Goose bumps ran up my arms and legs, not all due to the cold air blowing in behind Piper.

Louis stood directly behind me, breathing on my head. The two didn't speak and instinct suggested I might be in trouble. What kind, I hadn't a clue.

I tried to ease out of the middle of this danger sandwich. "I know Piper is a friend of yours, Louis. I'll leave you to chat. I need to get the sugar plums out to the guests. You know how cranky cops and firefighters can be when they don't get their sugar fixes. It'll be guns and fire hose time."

Louis' hand clamped down on my shoulder. "Yeah, hon, can you come back for me in a couple hours. The party should be over by midnight."

Piper's brow furrowed. "I thought you said nine o'clock. I came by earlier but some broad asked who I was instead of opening the door." She smirked at me and held out her nails. "How do you like the finished product?"

"Shut up, and wait for me outside," Louis told his girlfriend. "This is the police chief's wife."

"I know. We met this morning at the nail salon. Why can't I wait inside where it's warm?"

"Come back later," he pleaded.

Piper looked around the kitchen. "Where's the bag? I could take it now. We can leave right after the party." She seemed to remember I was there. "We're going away for the weekend."

Right. The primitive part of my brain engaged and I rammed my elbow into Louis' stomach. I could say I was sorry later if these two weren't villains.

Louis straightened, gasping for air. His head swiveled to take in the kitchen, and beyond to the party room. He stood between me and the door, so I edged slowly towards the sink area where there was a drawer that might hold knives, or at least a pizza slicer.

Louis saw me from the corner of his eye and turned, uncertainty and desperation in his eyes. I pulled the two-shelf wheeled trolley between us. Both shelves held plates of desserts, including a tray of the sugar plums.

"You should hit the road, Louis," I told him. "Beyond this kitchen are dozens of pumped-up cops and firefighters. Lots of testosterone flowing, as well as alcohol. What's going on?"

"Nothing. Where's the key to the media room?" His eyes darted from me to the alley, then at the entrance to the room-full of jacked-up first responders. With no warning, he shoved the trolley at me.

The sturdy metal cart overturned and knocked me to the floor. I landed against the wall, my right leg pinned under the wheels. Desserts sailed off the shelves, china smashing on the tiled floor. A few shards flew at me, and I felt a sharp pain above my left eye. My right thigh throbbed to the beat of my racing heart.

The pain slowed my brain enough to figure this out. "You're stealing the liquor supply. Are you crazy?" At a cop party.

"Only a few bottles. No big deal to the Wing Nut. It's a huge high, right under the noses of so many cops." Louis made up his mind. He grabbed a coat off a nearby table, but couldn't avoid stepping in the mess of broken glass and desserts on his way to the alley.

Piper stood open-mouthed, looking from me to Louis. "Where's your bag? And, the bottles?" Louis grabbed her arm and pulled her after him.

Footsteps pounded on the cement floor of the alley, headed our way. At the same time, Neil, Tony, and a posse of underdressed, off-duty cops piled into the kitchen. Glory's tall figure peered around their shoulders.

At that point, a whole lot of shit went down. Neil bent and flipped the trolley off me, while Glory's Valentinos slid on the dessert. Tony grabbed her arm and prevented her from face-planting, but I heard a knee hit the floor. She commenced her trademark howling while Tony lifted her onto the counter, away from trampling feet.

Uniformed cops from the alley dragged Louis and Piper back into the kitchen while the party-hearty cops and firefighters milled around getting in everyone's way.

"Get a couple of paramedics in here," Neil shouted.

"We're fine," I decided to speak for Glory since her mouth was engaged in screeching about her knee. A couple of sugar plums lay on my lap. I ate one. Sadly, most of the tray-full were crushed under the heels of too many shoes.

I straightened my right leg. The only part that hurt was the upper thigh where the trolley landed. I felt a moment's sympathy for Louis' mishap with my shopping cart at Canadian Tire yesterday. "Help me up," I said to Neil.

"Stay where you are. You're bleeding."

"Where? My face? Not my face!" I stayed put while a couple of paramedics, Jake and Freddie, shouldered through the crowded kitchen. I got Jake.

Apparently, paramedics don't bring their first aid equipment when they're off-duty at a party. Jake used paper towels to wipe the blood trickling down my cheek.

"Ah, here it is," he said comfortingly. "Just a little nick above your eye."

We both looked at my thigh. Jake raised one eyebrow and spoke to Neil. "I've ordered a couple of ambulances, just in case."

Neil leaned down and spoke in Jake's ear. Jake nodded and said, "Okay, Bliss, it's the hospital for you to get that cut stitched up."

That settled, I watched the uniforms hauling away Louis and Piper. "Catcha later, babes," I called after them. If you're going to be thieves, at least be good ones.

Most of the guests wandered back to the party. The bus wasn't leaving until midnight, so they might as well eat as much as possible. With Louis gone, the bar was closed. Sidebar: most of the liquor disappeared, but the bottles were accounted for. The town of Lockport paid for the stock sent from the Wing Nut.

As they rolled me from the debacle of a party, I saw the priest's rosy face peering between the crowd of well-wishers. I yelled at him, "Hey, Father. Did you know there's a goat in your nativity scene? Demons, you know?"

Catching sight of Fang and Chico just before the medics popped me into the ambulance, I called over, "Guys, can you bag a few dozen sugar plums for me? Yes, the purple-coated balls in the fridge."

Neil let go of my hand. "I'll follow you to the hospital."

I had more instructions to leave, but the ambulance door slammed shut. I was transported with no sirens and, for all I knew, no swirly lights. Okay, the hospital was three blocks away, but still.

Not So Silent Night

AT THE HOSPITAL, THE on-call doctor took me first due to my head injury. When Neil told her I was pregnant, she excused herself to make a call. She came back a few minutes later to say, "Dr. Reiner wants to see you. Fortunately, there's no concussion, but I'll order ice packs for your leg." She stitched up my head and left.

My leg had stiffened since the ambulance wheeled me into the ER. I shifted uncomfortably, and Neil's hand tightened on mine. His worried expression stopped me from asking about Louis and Piper.

I'd been changed out of my plum dress into an equally-drafty hospital gown. Fortunately, I didn't have to fight anyone to retain my underwear. The temperature of the examination room caused me to shiver uncontrollably. Neal took off his jacket and wrapped it around me. The warmth from his body engulfed me but l my legs hung free and turned goose-bumpy. Were warmed blankets a thing of the past in hospitals?

Dr. Ed Reiner, Neil's good friend, local coroner, chief of staff at the hospital — and my OB/GYN — threw the door open and strode in, looking down at me. I turned my head away.

"Well, what's happened, now?" He addressed Neil, used to my non-participation. At our appointments, he talked, I listened. I have an innate distrust of men who specialize in female parts and he was my doctor only because driving to the nearest small city to a woman gynecologist would be treacherous in the winter months. According to every woman in Lockport who gave birth under Ed Reiner's direction, he was the best. He'd better be.

I let Neil give him the Coles Notes version while I quivered in my scanty attire and wished I'd stayed out of the kitchen of the church hall and let Louis and his shady girlfriend steal the liquor. I'd be in my own warm bed by now. Actually, scratch that. I'd be cleaning up the hall, with Pan and Neil complaining non-stop.

Ed came at me with a phone-like device in one hand connected by a wire to a wand-shaped thing. He spread a cold, sticky gel over my abdomen and ran the wand over the area.

"This is a Doppler fetal monitor. At 12 weeks, I may or may not be able to detect the heartbeat. Try and relax."

It seemed like an hour, but likely only a couple of minutes before he turned off the monitor and ripped a strip of graph paper from a printer on the counter. "Well, I can definitely hear a good, strong heartbeat. I think you're farther along than 12 weeks. Maybe 16." He paused to let Neil and I consider that fact.

I looked at Neil. "That's before we were married."

He blinked at the bright lights over the cot. "Not possible. How did that happen?" He caught my eye and we laughed. Well, I laughed and his lips twitched up at the corners, a full-on guffaw from him.

"Why isn't she showing yet?" Neil asked Dr. Reiner. He peered at my stomach. I sucked it in.

"First pregnancy. Taut abdominal muscles. Anyway, everything sounds completely normal. I'm keeping you in overnight to be sure there are no effects from the head wound. I'll arrange an ultrasound in the next couple of days to verify an updated due date, but I see no reason to get a technician out of bed tonight."

He cleaned the gel off and reached into a cabinet for a cotton blanket. He tucked it around me. "Thank you,' I managed, shaking with cold and delayed reaction.

He said to Neil. "Help Bliss into the wheelchair, then find the duty nurse who will assign a room for the night. You can stay with her. Now, I'm going to look at Glory Yates' knee." He paused at the door and gave us a nod. "I don't see a thing to worry about, so both of you relax."

Oops, Glory. I hadn't given her a moment's thought since we were loaded into separate ambulances and whisked to the hospital. It was my fervent wish that her knee injury needed only a Band-Aid, or I'd never hear the end of it. Somehow, she'd blame it on me.

Without letting go of my hand, and he was hanging on a bit tight, Neil pulled out his phone. Not wanting me to hear, he turned his head and kept his voice low, but he forgot my bat ears, abused they may be. "Don't care. Keep them in separate cells. We'll sort out the charges tomorrow. I know they won't serve a day, but we can give them an uncomfortable night or two before they're bailed out."

A nursing assistant came in, slapped an ice pack on my thigh, and left again. "*Feliz Navidad* to you," I muttered as the door swung closed.

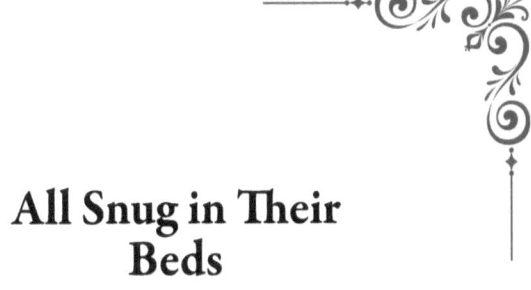

All Snug in Their Beds

THE PLASTIC MATTRESS under the thin sheet crackled every time I moved. The cold pack sent my core temperature even lower. Neil prowled the empty hallway until he found a linen closet and brought back three extra blankets. They helped, but I wanted something warm and cuddly on top of me. If it couldn't be my hunky husband, then the plush throw from our living room couch would be awesome.

Neil stood by the window and talked again in a quiet voice. He disconnected and told me, "I've asked Thea to stop at the house and take Bean for the night and pack a few things for you, including the fuzzy blanket from the couch. She'll drop the bag off at reception."

I patted his face. "You think of everything. Why did I resist you for so long when we first met?"

"You were making sure I wasn't just after your body." He recited the mantra and managed to look affronted after nearly two years.

"You were." That was for damn sure. He had to earn me. I made the man wait four months.

Neil took off his shoes and lay down beside me. I scooted over on the narrow bed so we'd both fit.

He bent over and kissed me, his body warming me more than four thin blankets. "You were worth the wait," he murmured, nuzzling the space behind my ear.

The door flew open, and Neil jumped from the bed. First to enter was a leg, the knee wrapped in a brace. The wheelchair and the rest of Glory appeared next. Tony followed behind, pushing his queen. Although, Glory didn't look much like royalty, garbed as she was in a hospital gown, her titian hair a mess, and no makeup.

"Have you got my phone?" I asked Neil. "I need a photo of this."

"Hi, roomie," she squealed. "My knee is sprained, not fractured. I insisted we share a room since we're both in for the night. Tony and Neil can stay, too."

So many things off about this. I whispered to Neil, "What did they give her for the pain. I want some."

He raised his eyebrows at me, then turned toward Tony who nodded at him with a grin I hadn't seen on his three-day-bearded face in weeks. I sensed undercurrents. Especially when Neil flashed a dimpled smile, maybe the third time since I met him, none of them aimed at me.

Glory prodded Tony. "Well, go ahead, hunkster. Tell them!"

Hunkster? "What's happening?"

The Detective-Sergeant helped Glory into bed, affording me a look at more of her than I wanted. I caught Neil blinking at her pink thong and bare back, and pinched his leg to re-focus him.

Joyful Tidings

THE HUNKSTER TUCKED Glory in all snugly and sat on the edge. He took her hand and reached across for mine. "We're pregnant. Fourteen weeks. With twins."

Glory squealed again. This time, I was ready for it and didn't flinch as much. "Awesome. Congratulations." One look at Neil's face and I knew this wasn't news to him.

"Why have you been so, um, serious the past few weeks?" I could say bitchy, mean, and hysterical. More than usual, I mean.

Glory composed herself. "They do more tests when they suspect twins. One of the tests initially showed there was a problem with one of the babies. They re-did it and Ed Reiner just gave us the results. Both babies are perfect. Isn't that super!"

"It really is. I'm glad everything is okay. By the way, I'm preggers, too. Sixteen weeks and, hopefully, one baby." I just wanted to get that out there in case Glory thought she was stealing the entire spotlight.

Glory looked surprised — okay, shocked was a more accurate word, but Tony exchanged proud smiles with Neil. So, my husband knew about Glory before this minute, and Tony knew about me. And, they say women can't keep secrets.

I glanced from Neil to Tony. "So, did you guys sit around one night while watching hockey, and come up with this super idea, like, 'Yeah, bro. What say we knock up our women?' Because you know how I feel about coincidences."

Glory's face lit up, another first. "Who cares how it happened? Isn't this fun? Next Christmas, we'll have three little ones running around the Christmas tree!"

I should nip this one in the bud. "Keep in mind, two of the wee darlings will be yours. I'll be chasing the one that looks like me. That's it."

Let's Take an Elfie

WHILE EVERYONE DIGESTED that thought, I had a brilliant idea. "This is a momentous occasion. We should take an elfie of the four of us. Get it? Elfie, not selfie."

The guys didn't want either one, but I hopped on my good leg over to Glory's bed, pulling Neil with me. Since he had the longest arms, I deputized him to snap a series of shots with my phone. I crawled back into my own bed and sent the photos to the other three.

Glory and I looked like the ghosts of Christmas past, with no makeup left on our faces, dishevelled hair, and clad in hospital gowns. I had the added bonus of a bandage over my left eyebrow. Glory surprised me and didn't demand do-overs after she did her face and hair.

"Ahh, aren't we all adorable?" She patted the mattress beside her. "Lie down here with me, baby. Oh, I guess I'll have to think of another pet name for you."

Tony rolled his eyes and lay on top of her sheets. Neither he nor Neil glanced at the photos. Neil flopped beside me and closed his eyes.

"You aren't lying on your gun, are you?" I was so freaking cold. "And, where's my coat? I don't remember having it in the ambulance." My dress and shoes travelled with me in the wheelchair in a clear, plastic bag.

"Sorry, your coat is still at the hall. I'll pick it up tomorrow. I gave my weapon to one of the off-duty officers to take to the station and lock in the gun safe. I'll get that tomorrow as well."

Neil had an office gun and a home gun which lived in our home safe. Usually. "You were expecting trouble, weren't you? That's why you brought your gun to the party."

"The owner of the Wing Nut asked for our help. For months, his inventory hasn't matched his sales. Louis is always keen for extra shifts, so the owner usually sends him to off-site gigs like tonight. He began to suspect Louis was taking more than he listed to these jobs and either taking them home to sell, or passing them on to someone else. Only a few bottles at a time, but it adds up. Turns out Louis and Piper have a history of ripping off their employers, and moving on before anything can be proven."

The door swung open and a nursing aide rolled in a cart. She handed Glory and me a fresh ice pack each and retrieved the old ones. If she disapproved of the double occupancy of both beds, she didn't mention it. "Which one is Bliss Cornwall?"

I waved at her, and she placed a small duffle bag at the foot of my bed. "A police officer dropped this off, and ..." She handed me a paper grocery bag. "Fang Davidson brought this in for you."

"Did you tell him I was fine?"

"We don't give out personal information to non-family." She pulled the cart from the room and closed the door.

I hobbled to the bathroom and shed the gown. With Neil's persistent help, I got into fleece pajamas, matching robe, and my bunny slippers. Back in bed, I sent Fang and Chico a quick text, letting them know everything was okay with me, and thanking them for their help this evening, adding that Chico should send me the photos he took of the three of us tonight. Except, where were they when I needed help? For that matter, where was my husband, sworn to protect and serve?

"That's why you didn't want to ride the bus. You were expecting trouble."

"I figured I might need my own vehicle. I'm sorry I didn't keep a better watch on you."

I started to roll over, then thought better of it. My thigh was purpling nicely, sort of divine retribution if you will, for inflicting a non-traditional colour scheme on the Christmas party. "So, you weren't ignoring me on purpose tonight?"

He rolled to face me. Sure, easy for him. "I would never ignore you, especially in a setting with both your ex-boyfriends from high school in attendance. And, a dress that short."

"They aren't ... never mind." He knew better but liked to tease me. He had a strange sense of humour. "You were expecting the booze thief."

"I can't apologize enough for not handcuffing you to my left wrist. You'd think I'd know by now not to let you run freely when a crime is about to be committed. You were hurt because I wasn't looking after you." He pressed himself closer to me.

Had he met me? When wasn't I in the thick of things? Not bragging or anything, more like complaining, but crap always happened even if I did nothing more than stand in a room. I was a freaking chaos magnet. I took his hand and murmured, "You always look after me but, next time, a head's up? I wouldn't have engaged Louis in friendly chit-chat if I'd known he was a suspect in a booze heist."

He snorted. "Hardly a heist, but I'll keep your request in mind for future stakeouts. Don't you want to rest, now? It's after two a.m."

In other words, he wanted me to shut up so he could sleep. Fine. I closed my eyes and I pulled my fuzzy blanket to my chin, making sure Neil was covered. My stomach rumbled and I sat up. The bag Fang dropped off. Where was it?

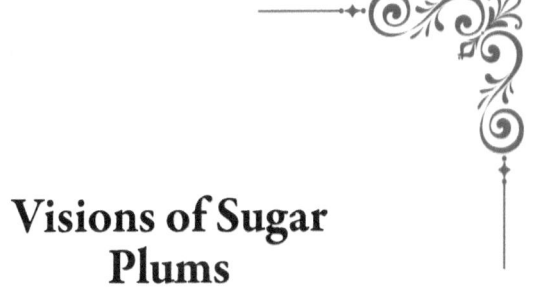

Visions of Sugar Plums

ON MY BEDSIDE TABLE. I opened the bag and looked in. I nearly teared up. Someone had taken the time to sort the desserts into separate baggies. Fang couldn't do that if he was given written instructions. Probably one of my own staff acting as a caterer tonight for extra cash. It didn't matter, I appreciated the thought.

I piled baggie after baggie onto my lap. Where were the sugar plums? Sure, they were delish, but there were hundreds of them. A few must have survived. I remembered the one I ate after it fell on my lap when I was pinned to the floor by the trolley.

Ah, here they were. At the bottom of the paper bag lay an extra-large baggie filled with sugar plums. I ate three before offering them around. "Sugar plum, anyone?" As in, one.

Neil pointed at his open mouth. I dropped one in. Tony stuck his large hand into the bag and came out with at least a dozen. "These are really good. Try and nibble on one, *mia amata*. The doctor said your calorie intake is too low. You're eating for three now."

"I guess I could try one." Glory's hand passed languidly over Tony's offering while she chose the perfect little ball. Like they weren't all the same.

Tony threw back a couple more and I fed Neil another. There was time before Christmas Day to order a few more batches from the bakery.

"Even my mama doesn't make anything as good as these," Tony said, reaching for another handful.

I resisted smacking his hand. Tis the Season. "Have as many as you like. Although ..." I did a quick estimate in my head.

"Wha...?" Tony asked through a mouthful, a layer of purple sugar dusting the bedding.

"Near as I can calculate, there's a chopped prune in every sugar plum ball. They shouldn't affect you unless you eat ten or more."

"I had probably 20 at the party." Tony looked at me like I'd poisoned him. "What's going to happen?"

Neil sat at the edge of the bed, chewing. "I ate at least a dozen there, and two here."

I laughed, sending a purple spray of sugar onto the floor. "I guess we know where you two will be spending tomorrow. Best leave the rest of these to two constipated, pregnant women."

"I'll take a couple more." Glory held out a hand and I gave her four.

Tony said to Neil, "Are we going to spend the next six months learning all about the changes in our wives' bodies?"

Neil spat the remnants of a sugar plum into a tissue and tossed it into the trash can. "I've read eight books on childbirth. I'm already traumatized and I haven't seen the videos yet."

"Wait," I said. My finger moved from Glory to Tony. "I heard you say the wife word. Did you guys slip away for a Vegas wedding in an Elvis chapel?"

The two exchanged knowing looks. "We're getting married the middle of January," Glory confided "You two are the first to know."

I let her reside in la-la land for a minute longer. Now that I knew she was pregnant, the tell-tale belly bump was unmistakable, especially on such a slender woman. I understood the voluminous, gorgeous dress she wore tonight. Make that last night. Another month, and the entire town would be alerted. Can't hide twins for long.

While Neil and Tony thumped each other's shoulders and bumped fists, the usual male primate behaviour, I said, "Um, so the Vegas thing is on for January?" Please, please, let it be so.

"No," Glory retorted. "Will you forget Vegas? We're having a small, intimate affair at the Country Club."

"Great!" I could get behind that. The club had their own venue coordinator. No reason for me to get involved.

"We'll talk next week," she confided. "Lots to plan. We need to discuss your odd colour preferences."

"Well, fu... Fudge." That reminded me. I ate another sugar plum.

"Why are there prunes in these things? Sugar prunes would be a better name for them," Neil said, thoughts of a coming wedding already gone from his mind.

Unbelievable. "What do you think prunes are before they're prunes?" I tapped his forehead. "Plums, my blond Adonis. Plums." I chose a plump ball from the bag.

Glory said to Tony, "You called Pan about bringing me some things for the night, didn't you?"

"Of course, I did, *mi amore*."

"He should be here. Can you find someone and ask? I'm so cold. I need my down wrap."

I didn't like the covetous look she gave my fuzzy blanket. I clutched it to my neck.

Tangled Tinsel

TONY DEPARTED TO OBEY his queen. The sugar plums made me thirsty and I doubted we'd get room service this time of night. I elbowed Neil.

Without opening his eyes, he said, "What?"

"Can you find us some drinks? I think I saw a snack machine down the hall."

That left me and the shivering Cranky Contessa alone. I edged to the far side of my bed so she couldn't reach over and snatch my blanket.

"I'm thinking white and silver would be good colours for my wedding," she said, dreamily. "What do you think, Bliss?"

"Well, *piccola patata*, neither of us will be terribly mobile for a week or two. I suggest we wait until after New Year's and work on it then." With any luck, she'd be rocking a significant tummy bulge and lose interest in a country club wedding. Maybe fly to Vegas.

"Did you just call me a potato?"

"A little potato. It's my new pet name for you. Like it?"

"No. Only Tony is allowed to talk to me in Italian."

Fortunately, both men came back, Tony with a black leather carryall, Neil with an armful of water bottles and juice cans.

With Glory changed and wrapped in her down-filled couch comforter, I thought we could all finally get some sleep. My brain wouldn't shut down. "I have to get out of here early and meet my teenagers at the hall to clean up. I hope they show." They would, all of them. I had a feeling.

"Already arranged," Neil murmured, pressed up against my back, his face in my hair. "I have Thea, two firefighters, and one paramedic meeting me at the church hall tomorrow. If the teenagers show up, they can help. I'll supervise and you stay home and rest."

I gave his thigh an affectionate squeeze. "You're so good to me."

Tony said, "I nearly forgot. The nurse gave me a note for you, Bliss." He pulled a crumpled sheet of paper from his pants pocket. "Father Hanley made her write this down verbatim. She wasn't pleased."

"Give it here." If the priest expected money to pay for the trashing, I'd just hand the message right over to Glory.

"Don't strain yourself, little lady. I'll read it to you." Tony chortled. "Are you ready? First item: The councillors left before 11 p.m., mostly sober. He ejected the drunks at midnight, and the bus left the parking lot at 12:10 a.m. He wanted to call the police to restore order, but then he remembered half the drunks were cops, and the other half consisted of firefighters and paramedics, with a smattering of bylaw officers. He sincerely hopes a catastrophe doesn't hit Lockport in the next 24 hours."

Neil groaned into my hair and breathed hot air onto my scalp. This is how we started out every night but, in our king-sized bed, I'd wait until he fell asleep — which took 30 seconds to a full minute — before crawling over him and sleeping on the other side. In this cot, I was trapped.

"His sermons must be real yawners," I said, "full of judgement and hell-fire. Anything else?"

"Oh, yes indeed," Tony expelled a full-out laugh, and Glory smiled watching him. "Next, everything in the hall is to be returned to its former state, exactly, by Tuesday afternoon which is Ladies' Bingo. Tomorrow evening would be even better. He underlined this one."

"Sounds fair. Okay, let's turn out the light now."

"Not done. This last thing is odd, but the nurse said she wrote down Father Hanley's words to the letter."

"Come on, Tony. Get it over with." Really, what more could there be?

"Of course, Miss Bliss. Apparently, goats are quite common in nativity scenes, but if you find hard evidence of devil-worship in his parish, please don't hesitate to inform him. Oh, and the nativity is to be returned to its rightful place in the foyer of the hall, without purple Santa hats, and the two errant wise men likewise." Tony turned the paper over. "That seems to be it."

"Wise men. That has to be the origin of the term oxymoron," I observed. "And, what's he trying to pull, here? Free labour? The nativity figures weren't in the foyer."

Glory emitted a strange noise, which scared me for a minute, until I realized she was giggling. That scared me more. "I'm so tired," she said, loudly enough that Neil woke up and looked around.

"Can we cut the lights and get some sleep," he complained.

Tony flipped off the fluorescent lights, plunging the room into darkness. Unable to get away from the heat of Neil's body, I threw off the plush blanket and hung my feet over the edge of the bed. "Hey, Glory, I've been thinking."

"Well, stop. I'm sleeping."

Loud snores erupted from the direction of her bed, probably Tony. I was grateful the night was half over. "I think we'll need to find another venue for the First Responders' Christmas Gala next year."

"Nothing gets by you, Bliss."

I reached for my bag of sugar plums. This was the best Christmas ever.

And to All a Good Night

APPRECIATION

HEARTFELT THANKS TO my longsuffering beta readers, Liz, Pam, and Maureen. They helped me reach a very short deadline for SUGAR PLUM BLISS, and not only offered valuable tips to make the story better but found typos my eyes missed. (So, if there are any left, it's not my fault. Just kidding! That was Bliss speaking through me, as she often does! Any errors are my own.)

My gratitude is boundless, my friends.

NOTE FROM THE AUTHOR

SUGAR PLUM BLISS is a Bliss and Neil Christmas special. FOR MORE OF BLISS MOONBEAM Cornwall and Police Chief Neil Redfern, check out the Cornwall & Redfern Mystery series, featuring small-town mystery, humour, murder, and more than a touch of romance.

Bliss takes sass to a whole new level as she kicks butt and takes no prisoners. Neil? He tries to contain the damage while solving murders and other crimes. Together, they're irresistible (if I do say so myself).

If you enjoyed SUGAR PLUM BLISS or any of the other books in the series, please consider leaving a review. That will make me dance for joy. Really, you should see me!

https://www.gloriaferris.com

gloriaferriswrites@gmail.com

A final note: For your reading pleasure, I have included the first chapter of DARK BLOSSOMING, Book 4 of the Cornwall & Redfern Mysteries.

Hope you like it.

ALSO BY GLORIA FERRIS

The Cornwall & Redfern Mysteries
CORPSE FLOWER
SHROUD OF ROSES
SKULL GARDEN
WEDDED BLISS (Novelette)
DARK BLOSSOMING
REAPER BLISS (Halloween Novelette)
The Mechanic Falls Gem Caper Series
By Ferris Tremain
(Gloria Ferris & Jamie Tremain)
WORLDS MAY CHANGE
TEQUILA CLAUS (A Christmas Special Novella)
WHERE WE STAND
The Blood Series (YA Contemporary Fantasy)
BLOOD PATCH
BLOOD SHIELD
The Blair & Piermont Crime Thriller Series
(with Donna Warner)
TARGETED
DEATH'S FOOTPRINT

ABOUT THE AUTHOR

GLORIA BEGAN HER WRITING career as a procedure writer at a nuclear power plant. Sure, it was an exciting job, but there's just so much you can do with prompts like, "Do NOT Press PB47," or "ACTIVATE the Evacuation Alarm and RUN!"

So, Gloria turned to fiction writing and is now the award-winning author of the humorous Cornwall & Redfern Mysteries; a co-written suspense series; and a YA contemporary fantasy series. As Ferris Tremain, she also co-writes the Mechanic Falls Gem Capers with author Jamie Tremain. Every so often, she'll write a short story just for the heck of it.

She has fully embraced her dark side but doesn't take it too seriously. She loves abandoned cemeteries, and all things "skull", managing to work one or both of these elements into her books. She once made an honest attempt to write a serious book, but that didn't go well, so now she lets her snarky and, occasionally, inappropriate humour prevail.

Gloria lives in southwestern Ontario.

DARK BLOSSOMING

A Cornwall and Redfern Mystery

Book 4

By Gloria Ferris

CHAPTER 1

THE AROMA OF MY SPICED latte was no match for Blackmire Swamp on a wet October afternoon. Just for context, if I was a super hero, my power would be smelling a decomposed raccoon months after it was digested by a vulture. The swamp smelled like that, but worse. I removed the lid of the take-out cup and stuck my nose in. Didn't help.

"Come on, troops." The leader of the expedition and, incidentally, the owner of the swamp, Chesley Belcourt, flipped his chin-length hair back, looking more like Lara Croft than Indiana Jones.

I wasn't keen on spending my afternoon following Chesley around, carrying the twigs he dug out of the stinky mud. My sack had to weigh five pounds already, and I wasn't adding one more *specimen* to my load.

I slouched along behind Chesley and Ciera as the path we'd taken into the swamp from behind the greenhouse disappeared into a water-logged, brown landscape. Even the half-drowned trees appeared defeated. Doubtful I'd find my way back if I made a run for it.

Chesley droned into Ciera's ear about the differences between swamps and marshes. Ciera listened politely as Chesley explained that swamps were full of trees while marshes were home to mostly grasses and other aquatic specimens. Shit, even I knew that. I lagged behind until his voice faded, but not so far as to lose sight of them.

Chesley stopped lecturing to ask me, "Bliss, did you deliver the Bat Flowers to local businesses as I asked?"

"Of course."

"Did you give them the instructions on the care of the plant and the flyer for my Halloween Gala?"

"Yes, Chesley." The black flowers were almost three feet tall, planted in appropriately-sized pots filled with heavy dirt. The owner of the Sweet Shoppe bakery had chased me to the door, shoving the plant back at me. The others took the plant but I could tell by their expressions the whiskery blooms were destined for an early trip to the recycling depot. "Everyone expressed their gratitude and promised to come to your gala thing."

His wide, gargoyle grin prompted Ciera to step behind and wait for me. She grunted with the effort of pulling each boot out of the sucking mud. "Are your rain boots designer, Bliss?"

"Coach," I replied, jumping over an evil mud hole. Reaching back, I grabbed her hand and pulled her through. She carried a few extra pounds and hadn't the option of leaping over puddles.

"You wore Coach to a swamp?"

"It's all I have." Ciera and Chesley wore black rubber boots from the greenhouse's stockpile, but nothing there fit my size fives. Moot point anyway — Bliss Moonbeam Cornwall did not wear footwear from a big box chain store.

My left boot and sock stayed firmly in the mud while my frozen toes fluttered in the dank air. "I swear by Lucifer's black ass, I will never step foot in this place again." Above me, a water-bloated tree shook icy raindrops on my head.

An hour into this safari, our boots were covered to the calves in thick, reeking sludge.

"They must've cost you a lot of money. I hope the mud will wash off."

I examined the dainty pattern on my boots. "These will never be clean again. I found a website where I buy most of my shoes and bags at a great discount. I can snag another pair."

"You mean the deep web?" Ciera's blond plait hung over her shoulder and glistened with moisture, the one bright splash of colour in this dismal place.

"No, I mean the dark web. Stay away from the deep web."

Ciera held the title of High Priestess of the Lockport Wiccan coven and owned a shop that sold esoteric items as well as crystals and books on occult subjects. Her coven celebrated the pagan holidays, and I can attest to the fact that some of these ceremonies were conducted with bonfires that you had to leap over while naked. I've observed it firsthand.

We returned our attention to Chesley as he emitted a hoot of triumph and dug into his backpack, his rear end encased in stretch jeans and vibrating like an excited bumblebee. He pulled out a fistful of small flags and stuck them into the ground around his feet. He handed Ciera and me a flag each. For a few minutes, he hopped around planting flags as though he had discovered an abundance of new continents. Ciera jammed hers randomly into the mud. I waved mine in support.

He called back over his shoulder, "These may be worth coming back for in the spring. Right now, I can't tell if they're *Ceratophyllum demersum* or *Larix laricina* saplings."

We three had different reasons for being in Blackmire Swamp on this Tuesday afternoon.

Chesley Belcourt was a crazy botanist. He had a passion for native plants and a mama rich enough to indulge his whims. Right now, as well as plans to propagate swamp plants, he'd purchased boxes of butterfly pupae on the cusp of hatching in the same steamy tropical greenhouse currently filled with black-blossomed plants for his Halloween display.

Ciera loved Chesley and he loved her. That explained her presence although I doubted she enjoyed long, romantic walks in a swamp.

It was all about the money for me. I worked for Chesley's mum, Ivy, at the Belcourt greenhouse complex five mornings a week, calling deadbeat customers around the world and encouraging them to hand over their credit card numbers.

Which didn't explain my attendance on this rare and endangered plant quest. Sometimes, Chesley required my help after the naughty customers on my list had surrendered. I refused unless he paid me the same generous rate I got from

Ivy. This gig consisted of Ches digging a root out of the ground, placing it into a baggie, and plunking it into my sack. Easy money.

Some people called me, "Anything for a Buck Bliss," but that's hardly fair. A girl had to support her designer habit and feed her investment fund. I couldn't expect my new husband to understand the thrill of the hunt for the perfect pair of Jimmy Choo pumps, even if that husband is the Chief of Police and hunts bad guys for a living. Before you argue that 7,000 citizens residing in Lockport on the shores of Lake Huron surely didn't require a police force of 21 constables, two sergeants, a deputy chief, and a chief, I refer you to the murders, drug busts, grave robbing, and gun-running that plagued this little slice of lakeside heaven in the last couple of years. Prior to meeting the adorable but stubborn Chief Neil Redfern, I had no idea so much crime thrived in Lockport.

Right this minute, I didn't care about money.

Moisture from the overhanging branches dripped down my neck. Other than shrill calls from birds, the sodden forest was quiet as a grave site. To reach the swamp, we had crossed River Road from the back of the greenhouse complex, pulled back branches to find the opening and entered a primal world where life first crawled out of the ooze. I'm not exaggerating. I once saw a movie that began in a setting exactly like this place where an eight-foot fish-man pulled himself out of a pit and searched the banks for a mate.

We'd passed Bird River, alive in the spring and summer with turtles, water birds, and — yummy — snakes. The deeper into the forest of twisted, half-drowned trees we trekked, the quieter everyone became. Ciera watched the treetops, her gaze flicking from branch to branch. A couple of turkey buzzards circled overhead. Ches stopped blathering about his wetland treasures and planted more flags.

Climbing over a branchy log, I caught a movement to my right. Back of the line wasn't a good place to be. "Hey, Ches, aren't reptiles supposed to be digging themselves into the mud for the winter?"

"Yes, most reptiles and amphibians have called it a day by now. They'll be at the bottom of the deeper mud holes."

A brown head reared up from a pile of wet leaves. "Including snakes?"

"Mostly."

Reassuring. "Then, what's this thing here?"

Ciera squealed and jumped behind Chesley. With his lady to protect, Chesley turned manly and squelched through the boggy ground to stand beside me. "That's a northern water snake. It's on a last hunt before winter."

I filed that information under my 'Check Google Later' file. Chesley was a botanist, not a biologist. I jabbed his chest. "Can we go now? I'm cold."

"We've been here an hour, and I haven't finished flagging plants of interest. In the spring I'll come back. Some of these plants will be worth transferring to the greenhouse for propagation."

Beside us, a bog pit 30 feet wide belched. A spurt of black sludge leaped into the air which became more rancid than before. If we stood here long enough, we'd die of swamp gas poisoning. "If I throw a match into the bog, will it light on fire?"

"Don't chance it." Chesley rammed a flag close to the bank to mark another unidentifiable gem. The snake crawled onto a wet log and watched us.

I looked away in time to glimpse Chesley's foot break through the eroding bank of the pit. I grabbed his jacket and yanked him onto firmer ground.

He fell onto his side, then scrabbled onto his hands and knees, swearing creatively. Consider me impressed. Until I realized he was riled with me for muddying his jeans.

"Next time, save yourself, idiot. For now, it might be a good idea to move away from the edge." I opened my shabby but still lovely Tory Burch tote and dropped in the empty coffee cup. The snake basked under the dripping trees on its log, flicking its tongue like it loved the taste of methane gas.

Chesley pulled his hands from the mud and reached back for his right boot. "Bliss, you're supposed to be helping me."

He made a move to crawl to safety and I hauled on his elbow, but he slid on the slimy ground. My knee connected with a rock jutting from the mud.

"Ow, ow, ow." I rested my weight on my other knee and waited for the pain to diminish.

"Big baby," Chesley muttered.

"Uh, wait a minute." I bent closer to the rock and pried away the mud. "This is an animal skull." I dug down as far as the eye sockets, then hesitated. "There's a jagged hole in it."

"Dig some more," Chesley encouraged, on his knees beside me. "I can use it in my Halloween décor."

Décor? I could charge him for props, over and above my usual hourly rate. A chill which had nothing to do with the temperature of the swamp ran down my spine, but I kept at it. Not until the upper jaw and teeth emerged from the mud did I stop and lean away.

"It's human."